"Sure to keep you on your toes. All the loose ends come to a close in a thrilling climax." —*Insite Magazine*

"There were heart-pounding, oh my gosh moments, some intense sabotage, and the writing was good, too!" —*Otakutwins Reviews*

"The Cruella DeVille of the year: that's who author Gay Yellen has expertly re-created as antagonist in The Body Business . . . one of those characters you just love to hate. And sticks with you long after the story ends." —*InD'Tale*

Praise for *The Body Next Door*

"A heartfelt, funny novel of suspense and romance, with a dead body thrown in. My favorite kind! Kudos to Ms. Yellen." —Pamela Fagan Hutchins, author of the bestselling series *What Doesn't Kill You.*

"Treat yourself to this romantic, vivid and skillfully-crafted mystery!" —Patricia Flaherty Pagan, author of *Trailways Pilgrims: Stories.*

"This is a true page-turner. I highly recommend The Body Next Door!" —Rebecca Nolen, best-selling author of *Deadly Thyme.*

THE BODY BUSINESS

A SAMANTHA NEWMAN MYSTERY

by

Gay Yellen

New 2020 Edition
ISBN 978-0-9978915-2-2

To Donald

CHAPTER ONE

The Message

O ne click. Just the slightest pressure of a finger, and her message would fly into the hands of the FBI. But it wasn't just any message. It would change Samantha Newman's life forever.

The cursor hovered over *Send*. So simple, and yet. She read the first part again.

Peculiar things are happening at De Theret International. High-level people disappear without explanation, and nobody seems to care. I am afraid who might be next.

It still sounded like the hallucinations of a conspiracy-theory nut job. Is that what she was, or was the danger real?

After a rough flight home, she'd spent most of the night hunched over the keyboard of her laptop, struggling for the right words. How ironic was it that she, the stellar young V.P. of Media Relations for the global staffing firm, couldn't write a simple e-mail?

Her eyes begged for sleep. If she weren't so jet-lagged, she could think more clearly. Maybe Lista *was* somewhere in South America, beyond the reach of a good phone signal, like their boss insisted.

For what seemed like the hundredth time, she called Lista's phone. And for the hundredth time came the same cheery greeting: "Hi! This is Lista. Sorry, but you'll have to leave a message."

Samantha pushed away from the table and paced the kitchen. A best friend would never just pack up, relocate, and not say goodbye. Not Lista, anyway, unless something was terribly wrong. She'd been missing for weeks.

With no evidence of foul play, the police had backed off. But Samantha knew better. Someone had to find Lista, before . . . before . . . what?

She searched the pocket of her robe for a scrunchie to hold back the curtain of auburn hair that had fallen across her face. No luck.

The tepid coffee in her mug wasn't helping. She eyed the pot, but its tar-like remains offered no solace. She turned it off and dumped the rest down the drain. Murky dawn crept through the window.

This is ridiculous, she thought. Stop being afraid. Put up or shut up. Get it over with.

She slumped down at the table again and scanned the rest of what she had written.

You must find out what happened to Lista Pearson, the last paragraph began. *Please, please help.*

It still didn't say all that it should, all that she knew. But she hoped it would be enough to get somebody's attention. If the FBI knew how much she hated asking anyone for help, least of all them, they would have to take her seriously.

The oven clock read six-thirty. Derek would arrive soon to pick her up, and she wasn't close to being ready. It was now or never.

Holding her breath, she sat up and reset the cursor over *Send*. This time, she didn't stop herself, and the message disappeared into the ether.

She stared at the empty screen, her pulse pounding in her ears. A jumble of thoughts bounced through her skull at warp speed. She closed her eyes until the mental roller-coaster stopped and she could open them again.

The kitchen looked familiar, yet something fundamental had changed.

Like the eerie hush that descends when the eye of a hurricane hovers, she was weirdly calm. The worst of the storm was sure to come. But for now, she had to drag herself upstairs and get ready for another dreadful day at the office, where the escalating hostility felt like a pair of clammy hands closing around her neck.

As Samantha stepped from the steamy cocoon of her shower, the doorbell rang. So much for the extra time she took under the hot pulsating spray, trying to unclench her muscles. Everything re-clenched at the sound of the bell.

She wrapped herself in a towel and opened the door to her bedroom. The cool dry air gave her goose bumps.

She was halfway across the room when the radio kicked on. "This is Goo-oo-ood Morning Radio! Let's wake up, Houston!" It might as well have been a gunshot.

Her heart raced. She stubbed her toe and nearly fell over the half-unpacked suitcase she'd left on the floor last night.

Whoa. Get a hold of yourself. She rewrapped the towel and glanced at the clock: six-fifty. The doorbell rang again.

Drat. Derek wasn't supposed to pick her up until seven-fifteen. How like his exasperating self to be early, especially this morning.

"Okay, okay!" She raced barefoot down the stairs. "I'm coming!"

Still damp and goose-bumpy, she peered through the door's peephole. The tanned, handsome face smiling back at her was indeed Derek Grey's. She wrapped the towel tighter and cracked the door, a little wider than she'd intended. Too wide.

His dark eyes traveled over her nearly naked body, following the tiny rivulets of water that trickled down her bare neck and chest toward her cleavage.

She flushed. *Should've put my robe on.*

"May I come in?" He crossed the threshold without waiting for an answer. Derek, back in her house. Bad idea.

His eyes swept the room. "I see things haven't changed much."

She winced. "It's only been a week since you moved out. Hardly enough time for a major redo."

"Oh, sure. You're probably still mourning the loss."

She wished she could tell him how true his little joke was. "This hasn't been easy for either one of us."

"Then why'd we do it, Sam? That part's still a little fuzzy to me."

The hurt in his voice twisted her heart. "Please, Derek, let's not do this again. Just leave me here and go on to the office. I'll catch a ride myself."

He held up his hands in surrender. "Okay, I get it. I'm only a friendly co-worker, giving you a lift to work 'cause your car died, for like, the millionth time."

"Thank you." At least he was trying.

He made a second visual tour of her damp body. "Looks like I have some wait time. Any coffee left?"

He made a move for the kitchen.

The image of her laptop, still open on the kitchen table, sparked in Samantha's brain. She stepped into his path to stop him. They bumped into one another with only the towel between them, and for an awkward moment, their eyes met.

She backed away. "Coffee's all gone."

"I'll just make some fresh and wait for you. Like the old days." He flashed one of his killer smiles.

"Please go to the office without me, Derek. I shouldn't have let you pick me up in the first place."

"Not to worry, my sweet. I know I'm a little early.

I'll just chill with my coffee in the kitchen."

"I'll make the coffee. Go sit on the sofa and I'll bring it to you." She ignored the hurt look on his face and hurried to the kitchen to grab the laptop.

To her chagrin, Derek followed. He eyed the laptop as she slammed it shut. "What're you working on?"

"Nothing. Just wanted to make some notes for a new idea while it's still fresh in my mind."

"Wanna share?"

"Not yet."

He shook his head. "You do love your secrets."

How could she tell him that she couldn't confide in anyone at work right now, including him? "Look, I had a long day in New York yesterday, and a hellish flight home. I'm a little cranky, I know. I just need some space right now."

She lifted her briefcase from the chair and dropped the laptop inside. "I'm going upstairs to get dressed. Stay or leave. I don't care."

"In that case, I'll make myself some coffee. It's not like I don't know where everything is around here."

Without the energy to argue, she turned to go. "I'll just be a few minutes."

She retreated to the stairs with her briefcase. At least temporarily, Derek was off the scent.

Samantha threw on her stand-by gray suit, finger-combed her damp hair and returned downstairs as fast as she could.

When she reappeared in the kitchen, Derek smiled. "Is it okay for just-a-friend to say that you look gorgeous this morning? As usual, I might add."

In trying to be a good sport, Derek was making it hard to keep him at a distance. Especially now, when she missed his buoyant spirit the most.

She willed herself to lighten up. "Thanks for the compliment, but I feel like a hundred-year-old hag today."

"Well, you don't look a day over ninety-nine to me."

Again with the charm. If only he wouldn't speak to her, ever. If only he hadn't gotten so chummy with their boss, Vinson De Theret. If only she could still trust him.

"Better bring an umbrella," Derek advised. "It's raining. That reminds me . . ."

He pulled a garage door opener from his pocket and held it out to her. "I parked inside your garage just now, so we wouldn't get wet. But since you took my house key, I figured you'd want this too."

She stared at the device, the last vestige of their shared life. When she took it from him, the brief touch of his hand sent her deeper into regret.

Breaking up was supposed to be the hard part. But what do you do if he never really goes away? She opened the utility closet to retrieve an umbrella, relieved that he couldn't see her face.

Samantha stared past the clacking windshield wipers of Derek's Cadillac, becoming increasingly irritated at herself for accepting his offer to drive her to work. At least it was raining. Sunshine would be too much to deal with today.

Derek was happily detailing the particulars of the account he'd just signed, a big drilling firm. He loved his job at De Theret International. Mercifully, she was only expected to listen.

"When will your car be ready?" he asked.

"Later today, I think. They had trouble getting the right part."

"Cheap foreign cars," he said as he steered his car smoothly through the rain.

"A Corvette is not foreign. Or cheap."

"Oh, right. It's been so long since I drove your car, I forgot."

Her last nerve snapped. She grabbed the dashboard. "Stop!"

He jammed on the brakes. The car skidded on the wet pavement. Luckily, Derek steered it to a halt at the curb without hitting anything.

He gaped at her. "What happened?"

"This was a bad idea. We shouldn't be doing this."

He pounded his hands on the steering wheel. "Good grief, Sam! I thought we were about to get slammed by a two-ton truck or something."

"Let me out. Please." She gathered her briefcase and umbrella, ready to leave.

"In the rain? C'mon, I was only razzing you about your flaky car. Why are you so touchy this morning?" He checked the mirrors and steered into an opening in the traffic.

At the next red light, she opened the door to get out. Rain pelted her skirt. Ankle-high gutter water swirled at her feet.

"Are you crazy?" he yelled. "Get back in here!"

Faced with certain drenching, she pulled her feet inside and shut the door.

When the light turned green, Derek hit the accelerator hard. The car hydroplaned a few feet before he regained control. "Don't do that again. Please!"

"Let's just not talk, okay?"

A few blocks later, Derek broke the silence.

"I won't be around at lunch today, in case you were counting on my trusty chauffeur service to take you somewhere elegant. I'm playing tennis with De Theret."

Her stomach clenched at the mention of their boss, Vinson De Theret.

A speeding truck doused her side of the car in a tsunami of water. "Indoors, I presume," she muttered.

"His club, actually. The ol' Rabbit still insists he can beat me, and I may let him do it this time. It's not nice to bloody one's boss as regularly as I have. What do you think?"

"Uh-huh."

Samantha's mind was on De Theret, the person that Derek had secretly nicknamed "The White Rabbit" the day she introduced them. It was the perfect moniker for the squat man, with his pale, permanently bloodshot eyes, nearly colorless hair and repertoire of facial tics that made him seem ready to bolt for cover. A strange quality in a successful businessman like De Theret, but whatever haunted his psyche was likely the same thing that drove him to want to win, and win big.

Derek's voice snapped her back to the present. "You are miles away, aren't you?"

"I guess I'm not quite awake."

"Or not interested."

The light turned red. He stopped and turned to her. "Are you still obsessing about Lista?"

She felt the familiar laser beam of his focus. Unable to manufacture a convincing response, she stared ahead.

The traffic light changed. They were rolling again, but his attention stayed on her.

"You are hell-bent on losing your job, aren't you, Sam?"

"Look, Derek—"

"No, you look. You've got a stubborn streak a mile long, and a crazy misplaced feeling of responsibility for Lista—"

"It isn't misplaced. You of all people know what I owe her."

"You don't owe her your career, and that's what you're risking here, hounding everybody about where she is. Vinson's just about had it with you."

She gaped at him, trying to fully grasp what he meant. "He told you this?"

"No, but I see the look on his face when your name is mentioned. Lista may be your friend, but you know she's a disaster waiting to happen. So you haven't heard from her, so what? She gets herself in trouble every other day over some stupid little thing—"

Samantha pounced. "You think she's in trouble?"

"No, she's not in trouble. She's in Colombia, like Vinson says."

"How do you know?"

"Here we go again." Derek shook his head. "Honestly, Sam. You're the one who got me to quit that albatross of a law practice I was stuck in and try a new gig at your company. But since we've been working at the same place, we keep moving farther apart. I can't help it that the Rabbit likes me. It was your idea, remember?"

Yes, she wanted to say, I remember. And now, I regret.

No point arguing about Lista. It always turned out the same. "Sorry," she said. "I'm not enthralled with our boss lately. I'm sure it's just a phase. Hope you beat the pants off him today."

He seemed satisfied with the apology. Only the clack of the wipers and the ziss of the wet pavement filled the silence.

She longed to tell him that this wasn't only about Lista. Other key people in the company had dropped from sight months before, and the latest quarterly reports boasted numbers that didn't add up. Derek had been her rock through the toughest of times. But lately, to further his own success, he had chosen a side, and it wasn't hers.

Samantha needed answers before her own career, her whole life, went up in smoke. Maybe she was paranoid, and all was okay at De Theret International. Maybe Lista would turn up soon, and things would get back to normal.

Maybe then she could explain everything to Derek, and he would understand. Even if it was too late for forgiveness.

His voice interrupted her reverie. "Your place or mine?"

She felt her heart twist again. "What?"

She'd been so deep in thought, she hadn't noticed that they were approaching the last turn into the De Theret parking garage.

Derek pointed to the parking slot ahead of them. "Your space is closer to the elevator. Shall I park there?"

"Whatever you want, Derek."

"Wish that were true, my dear." He eased his car into her reserved space. "Wish it were true.

CHAPTER TWO

The Bureau

Mack Maginnis walked down a narrow hallway inside the Houston office of the FBI, a steaming mug of coffee in one hand and a doughnut in the other. For weeks, he had observed the odd behavior of one of Homeland Security's top consultants. Today, he was determined to confront him.

At the end of the hall, Maginnis stopped to scan the large open space filled with work modules. There, on the far side of the room, sat the person he was looking for: Carter Chapman, ex-NSA cyber-espionage expert.

Chapman's analytical software had been installed at the bureau a few months back. As promised, it exposed convergences of previously unrelated threads of data, which helped solve more cases, faster. Lately though, Chapman's presence set off the veteran agent's radar. Something weird was going on with the guy.

Tall, good-looking, with earnest brown eyes and a thick head of hair, Chapman could play the perfect hero in a Hollywood movie. He didn't seem like the kind of guy in need of a cubicle. Yet he'd been at the Bureau almost every day for a couple of weeks now, working at one of their computers, and nobody could explain why.

Maginnis slipped into his affable office demeanor as he entered the cramped module. "Hey, fella, how are ya?"

Chapman snatched a thumb drive from the side of the computer, dropped it into the pocket of his denim shirt and closed the file on the screen.

Maginnis pretended not to notice as he lowered his once-svelte body into the chair beside the desk. "Whatcha doin' here this mornin'?" He took a sip from his mug and waited.

Chapman kept his eyes on the blank screen. "Just checking on the convergence model we installed for you. Making sure it's running smoothly."

"We're having problems with it?"

"Uh, no, but I want to make sure that you don't."

Unconvinced, Maginnis bit into his doughnut and chewed it slowly.

"This is part of your contract," Chapman added. "I'm not trying to pad the bill, or anything."

"Didn't think you were. It's just that you're still hanging around the house, even though our date was over weeks ago, far as I know. Something else you're doing for us?"

Chapman didn't respond. Maginnis tried again. "Can you show me what you're working on?"

"Why?"

"Just curious."

They quietly assessed one another. Maginnis finished his doughnut and coffee while Chapman randomly opened and closed programs on the screen.

The agent tried another tack. "You know, Chapman, all of us here appreciate the work you've done for us. Heck, I've used your program myself a few times, and darned if it didn't practically round up the bad guys and throw them into the slammer all by itself. I mean it. That thing's slicker than owl poop."

"Thanks."

"You're welcome."

If Chapman wanted to end the conversation, he was free to leave, which Maginnis half-expected him to do. But he stayed in his chair. Maybe he'd open up after all.

"Here's the thing, buddy. I can't figure out why you keep coming back here all the time. I mean, pretty soon, we'll have to give you a badge and a gun, 'cause it looks like you've got nothing better to do than lurk around our hallowed halls."

"I'm not lurking."

"Then what is it, exactly, that you're doing here? Don't you have other clients you could beam yourself up to?"

Chapman drummed his fingers on the keyboard.

Maginnis dialed back his natural tendency to ratchet up the pressure. "I'm just sayin', pal, you look like the cat that swallowed Mrs. Ortega's canary. In my book, that makes you kinda suspicious looking. And I don't take you for a squirrelly kind of guy.

Nobody else seems to know what you're doing here, so I figure if I ask you straight up, you'll give me a straight-up answer. How 'bout it?"

Chapman swiveled away from the desk and looked directly at Maginnis. He seemed to be weighing his options.

"Okay," he said at last. "Maybe it's time I told somebody about this. I could probably use some help on the project myself."

"Project? So, you're still working for us?"

"Well, not really a project. More like a personal quest."

"Quest?" Maginnis echoed. "You mean like the Holy Grail?"

"No."

"How 'bout I start with what I know," Maginnis offered. "You've still got top security clearance, so that's a point in your favor. I know you were a major NSA cyber-celeb before you left and started your mega-successful consulting company. You've been a solid contractor with us. But I can't figure out why you're still here. And right now, you're looking at me like there's something serious on your mind. So, what gives?"

"It's nothing. A personal issue, really. I'm here because . . ." Chapman stopped and started over. "My ranch isn't too far, just a short drive from the city, and I needed to—" He took a deep breath.

Maginnis squelched the urge to throttle the guy. The way things were going, this little *tete-a-tete* could take all day. Close to losing patience, he pulled a phone from his pants pocket and checked for messages, reading and deleting e-mails, and waiting.

Chapman finally broke. "Okay here's the thing. I, uh . . . I've been using my system, the one I installed here, to do a little, um . . . detective work of my own. But I don't think I've broken any laws."

Maginnis returned the phone to his pocket. "I'll be the judge of that,"

A guy with Chapman's background could have said that the work he was doing was classified above the agent's pay grade, and that would have been that. But he didn't, and the sadness that swept across the man's face led the agent to believe he was on the level.

Maginnis stood. "Tell you what. I could use more coffee. Why don't you come with me to my office where we have more privacy, and we'll grab some joe on the way. Okay?"

His thoughts were abuzz with possibilities as he waited for Chapman to turn off the computer. The day had barely begun, and already it looked to be very interesting.

CHAPTER THREE

A Business Proposition

As Samantha and Derek waited for the elevator, she caught sight of E.B. Odom approaching them with her usual hip-swaying saunter.

Freshly enhanced from yet another plastic surgery, salon-coiffed and expensively tailored, E.B. bore little resemblance to her former self: Miss Eula Beth Bewley, the dry stick of a bumpkin who started at De Theret the same day as Samantha.

Over the years, E.B. had clawed her way over hapless co-workers to the top echelon of executives. She had also managed to kill off all remnants of the old Eula Beth, except for the stiletto heels and the long fingernails, now lacquered blood-red and featuring a diamond imbedded in the right index talon.

"Good morning, you two." E.B.'s giggle sounded more like a viper's rattle. She slipped her arm through Derek's and smiled up at him.

"My goodness, Derek, what did you do to our friend this morning? She looks positively ravished!"

Her focus slid toward Samantha. "Poor Miss Newman, it's obvious to me from her sad little face that you're much too much for her. She should have sent you to me sooner. I know how to handle bad little boys. Part of the job, you know."

Samantha shrank into a corner of the elevator, wondering why everything E.B. said sounded so blasted slutty. She tried to concentrate on the numbers above the elevator door as they lit up, trying to speed them telepathically. Newly unattached as Derek was, she hoped he wouldn't succumb to E.B.'s obvious come-on.

At last, the doors opened, and the trio got on. Samantha pushed four, Derek, three.

"I'm coming with you this morning, Derek," E.B. purred. She squeezed his arm and looked at Samantha, a challenge in her eyes. Her office was on the executive fourth floor, just down the hall from Samantha's. But she seldom missed an opportunity to flirt with Derek, or most any man, for that matter.

"Get off, E.B.," Samantha said, icicles dripping from each word.

"I beg your pardon?"

"This is three."

"Oh, so it is!" E.B. giggled again. "Come Derek. Come play with me." She tugged him out of the elevator. "Your old girlfriend's no fun anymore."

He offered an apologetic glance over his shoulder and followed E.B. out.

As soon as the doors closed, Samantha took a long, deep breath. By the time they opened onto the fourth floor, she was ready to chew tacks.

E.B. followed Derek into his office. "I know you have work to do," she cooed. "However, I think you'll like my little jump start to your day. I'm here with good news."

"No problem." He felt more favorable than usual toward E.B. this morning. Samantha's rejection still smarted. Why wasn't she happy that he was Vinson De Theret's new star employee.

E.B.'s little game at Samantha's expense had made him feel better. Besides, being nice to the V.P. of the Elite Professionals division could have its benefits. He set his briefcase down behind his desk and took the chair, waiting for the woman's next move.

E.B. shut the door and locked it, then dropped her Gucci tote onto a chair and sashayed up to Derek's desk.

He couldn't help but assess her physical attributes. While Samantha downplayed her own natural beauty, E.B. used every artifice to fabricate an aura of voluptuousness, and not without success. Her legs, while thin, were long and reedy, and her hips, though narrow, bore the promise of readiness when she walked. Her surgically augmented breasts, firm and unfettered by any undergarment, struggled against the confines of her thin silk blouse: a pair of ray guns set for stun.

Few women could compete with such physical artillery, and few men could resist its mesmerizing effect. All this, topped by a face well-practiced in the art of the come-hither look, and framed by a mane of improbable platinum hair, produced an affectation of sexuality akin to that of a life-sized Barbie doll: plastic, but a tantalizing approximation of the ideal.

Once again, she measured him with her amber eyes. A slim leg emerged from the deep slit in her well-tailored skirt. She perched it across a corner of his desk.

His gaze traveled up her thigh. He could almost feel the silky smoothness of her skin. It had only been a few days, but it seemed like an eternity since he had been with Samantha. He was not used to being alone.

"I'm going to tell you some things that are very, very confidential," E.B. said. Her eyes bore into him from under her heavy lashes. "But before I do, I need to know something."

Derek shrugged. "My mind is an open book," he said, trying for a smile. "What do you want to know?"

"I need to know that it's over, really over, between you and Samantha."

"She kicked me out," he replied. "And even though I don't understand why she did it, I know Samantha. Once she makes up her mind, she stands by her decision. She'll never take me back."

"Silly girl. But what about you?"

"I don't look back, either. If it's a matter of trust, whatever you say to me will never get back to her. I swear it on those gorgeous tiger eyes of yours."

Derek knew that E.B. would swallow the compliment. He also knew he could play any game of her choosing and, at worst, come out even. She might be able to intimidate most people, but she was still a woman. His history with the fairer sex told him the odds were on his side.

E.B. held him in her gaze and smiled. "I'm offering you a promotion, Derek."

She had his attention now. He sat up.

"There are things going on at this company that even Samantha doesn't know about. Big things. Very confidential things. We think you have a lot of potential to develop some new areas for us, but we want you to be free of Samantha. To be your own person, so to speak, before we invite you in."

"We?" He had assumed whatever E.B. had in mind involved an intimate twosome.

"Vinnie and me."

E.B. and Vinson De Theret. So, this was a business proposition.

"We like you, Derek," she continued. "We like Samantha too, of course, and we're grateful to her for bringing you into the company. But you don't need her anymore. You can stand on your own now. With my help, of course."

He sifted through the shards of innuendo she'd handed him. A mix of possibilities played in his brain.

E.B. had confirmed what he had only guessed at before. There was some kind of special relationship between her and Vinson De Theret, one that gave her more real power than Samantha had, even though the two women were equals on the organizational chart.

He was well on his way to gaining the Rabbit's confidence. One more ace in the hand wouldn't hurt.

Yet, E.B. had sensed the depth of his ambition, and it unsettled him. He was starting over in a new career, and at thirty-six, his youthful energy was threatening to slip away. This could be his last grab at the brass ring. He would do anything to get to the top of the company, where the real action was.

He resented E.B.'s suggestion, however veiled, that he had used Samantha to get ahead at De Theret. But after their breakup, he had feared that he wouldn't reach his goal without her. Now, he saw another way.

He smiled. "I'm all yours, E.B."

"All in good time, love. Consider this the preliminary interview. In the meantime, I want you to stay close to Samantha."

She leaned down from her perch to stroke his hair. Her perfume enveloped him in a cloud of bergamot. Its bitter undertone reminded him of the gum his great-grandmother chewed to get rid of a toothache.

He pulled away. "But I told you, Sam and I are through. She doesn't want me around."

"I know what you said," E.B. cooed. "But it shouldn't be too difficult to get her to have a drink with you now and then. You know, for old times' sake. After all, the management team must stick together."

She leaned in and stroked his hair again with her long crimson nails. "You know," she said softly, "Samantha and I don't always communicate well, one-on-one. It's important to me that you keep me informed about what she's up to."

Derek wasn't sure he liked where the conversation was headed. Just because he'd said it was over with Samantha didn't mean he would stop caring about her. What exactly was E.B. asking him to do?

"I promise you'll like this job," she purred. "It has lots of fringe bennies."

He recognized the cues: her exposed thigh, her breasts rising ripely from the scoop of her blouse. Whatever else she wanted from him might be puzzling, but this invitation was obvious.

He stood and pulled her up hard against his body. If she didn't want it this way, she could still protest. But there was no resistance.

"Just tell me what you want me to do," he breathed in her ear.

She molded her torso to his. "You know what I want," she hissed. "Make me happy. Give me what I need, and I promise, you'll be very happy too."

This time, there was no hesitation. Whatever else she might ask of him, this was an assignment he knew how to handle.

CHAPTER FOUR

Speechless

Gertrude Gold stood at Samantha's office door with a black coffee and a home-made sunrise muffin. She exchanged the mug and muffin for Samantha's briefcase and followed her inside.

"You're a lifesaver, Gertie. How do you always manage to know what I need?"

"I'm a good guesser. Besides, I know how hectic your schedule in New York was. Are you okay?" Gertie's motherly tone bore genuine concern.

"Fine. Why?"

"You look kind of puffy, like you're still hauling your travel bags . . . under your eyes. At my age, they could pass for high cheekbones. But on you?" She chuckled at her own joke.

Gertie's cheery, maternal nature was what Samantha loved most about her. When the plump, fifty-something widow first showed up for the job interview, more than a few eyebrows were raised. She didn't fit the mold of De Theret's Elite Professionals— the young, svelte, cookie-cutter-chic executive assistants who were the company hallmark.

"Not really our type," Vinson De Theret had commented.

But Samantha won the debate to hire her. De Theret could have his beauty queens. Samantha would gladly keep her capable and loyal Gertie.

Gertie followed Samantha into her private office and set her briefcase beside the desk. "Anything else you need?"

Samantha took a sip of coffee and booted up her computer. "Yes. Get Karen Plummer on the phone for me, please. I haven't heard from her about the speech I'm supposed to give next week at the National Council of Business Women's Conference."

"Will do, boss."

Samantha had barely taken a bite of muffin before Gertie's voice piped through the intercom. "I've got Karen Plummer on one."

She swallowed and picked up the phone. "Hello, Karen. Glad I finally reached you."

"Samantha! You are one busy lady!" Karen Plummer's husky alto was unmistakable.

"I could say the same for you."

"Listen, I was sorry to hear you have a conflict with our conference date. Kinda hurt my feelings."

"I . . . what?"

"Your other speaking engagement?"

Samantha's mind raced, trying to catch up to what Plummer was talking about.

"I called yesterday to discuss the topic of your speech with you," Plummer explained. "Your secretary was at lunch, and whoever I spoke to said you were out of town. They referred me to E.B.

Odom. She said you'd probably have to cancel because you had some other thing going on at the same time."

"What other thing?"

"Don't you know?"

Samantha was at a loss.

"Anyway," Plummer continued, "I was in a real bind, because the program was being printed that day, and I needed a speaker and a topic ASAP. Luckily, E.B. said she'd done a talk last year for Working Women of America called 'How to Get Promoted' and she'd be happy to do it for us. A real lifesaver. I only hope she's as good as you are."

It suddenly felt like millions of E.B.'s sharp claws were poking her from all sides. She could barely push words past her clenched teeth.

"I can still do it for you, Karen."

"Would that you could, sweet. But I had to go to press with the program last week. Wait! You mean you don't have a conflict? Was E.B. mistaken?"

"No, she was . . ." Samantha cleared her throat and swallowed hard. "She wasn't mistaken."

"I'm sorry it didn't work out," Plummer said. "Maybe next year?"

"Listen Karen, I'm sorry. I've gotta go. I'll, uh . . . talk to you later." Samantha hung up without bothering to say goodbye. Her mind was spinning.

Anger, she knew how to control. Even rage could be channeled into positive action. But tired as she was, she felt helpless against E.B.'s unrelenting onslaught. And helpless was not a feeling she liked.

Their very first confrontation years ago came flooding back.

Back then, E.B. was Eula Beth Bewley, a girl from a small town in the bleak, dusty flats of West Texas. She'd started her entry-level clerical position at De Theret International on the same day that Samantha entered the management training program.

On the job barely a week, E.B. had invited Samantha to go for a happy hour chat after work. Making friends with as many people as possible at the new company seemed like a good idea, so they agreed to meet at a nearby hotel bar after work.

Eula Beth ordered a rum and cola. Samantha opted for wine.

When the drinks came, Samantha watched as her bar mate plunged a fingertip, enameled in iridescent sparkles, into her cocktail to stir the ice. Then she sucked her finger dry.

"Goll-ee, Miss Newman," Eula Beth drawled. "I'm so glad you want to be friends and have a drink with me, 'cause you and I are gonna lock horns, if we're not just a teensy bit careful." She finger-stirred her cocktail again.

"I'm sorry?" Samantha searched Eula Beth's face for the meaning of her comment. "And call me Samantha, please."

"C'mon, Miss Newman. Samantha. Like my momma used to say, you're not as dumb as you look.

I've watched you. You're smart. And pretty. And you think you can go somewhere in this company. And maybe you can. But not at my expense." Eula Beth's eyes narrowed under their heavy load of mascara. "So stay the heck away from Trey."

"Trey? Trey Odom?"

Samantha wondered what she had done to prompt the threat. She'd had one brief conversation with him in the company cafeteria. Being a fresh trainee, she could hardly have captured much notice from the head of the South American division.

"Don't go playin' all innocent, now," Eula Beth continued. "I've seen you around him, actin' all interested and hard-workin' and offerin' to stay late to get some so-called work done. And I'm tellin' you, he's mine, so don't go hornin' in on my deal."

"Yours?" Samantha lowered her voice to keep it from carrying to the next table. "Eula Beth, he's married!"

"So?" The secretary's expression could have iced a Houston sidewalk in July.

Samantha reconsidered the person sitting across from her. Eula Beth looked every bit the small-town floozy, from her spike-heeled sandals to her oversized hoop earrings and aggressively teased, streaked and frosted hair. With her miniskirt stretched tightly over her hips, and the buttons on her blouse straining against her amply padded bosom, she seemed poised to split an old, useless skin, with a fearsome predator waiting to slither out.

The intercom snapped Samantha back to the present.

"If you don't mind, I'll be going to lunch a little early today," Gertie's voice chirped. "Want me to bring back something for you?"

"No thanks. My stomach's a little unsettled this morning. The muffin should tide me over."

"Well, I'm not leaving for another hour or so. I'll check with you then."

Samantha smiled. Everyone else in her life may be drifting away, but Gertie remained steadfast. With Lista missing, and Derek at arm's length, at least there was still one person who had her back.

Piles of work confronted her, but her mind was not on the job. She itched to confront E.B. about stealing her speaking date at the women's conference. But more than anything, she wanted to find Lista.

It seemed like days, not hours, since she'd sent that message from her kitchen. Had anyone at the FBI read it yet?

CHAPTER FIVE

The Gift Horse

Carter Chapman's confession in the privacy of Maginnis's office had convinced the agent of two things.

One: his instincts were right. The guy definitely had bent a few rules and used FBI resources for help with a personal matter. And Two: his story was compelling.

Though he might be a little slow to warm up to, Chapman was basically sincere. And the personal matter he was working on had the potential to become a career-maker for an enterprising agent.

The next morning, when the new tips and queries from the public access site were delivered to his desk, Maginnis discovered that fate had dropped a lucky break in his lap. In no time, he found Chapman at his cubicle.

"A message from heaven," Maginnis announced, waving the report in the air.

Chapman grabbed the papers. A few pages in, he laser-focused on the highlighted item. A person named Samantha Newman was looking for a missing friend.

He sat up. "This is great news. I'll clear my calendar and—"

"Whoa there, buddy," Maginnis said. "This is an FBI case, and, as previously discussed, you are not one of us."

"There's no way you'd even know this was case without me!"

Maginnis put a hand on Chapman's shoulder to quiet him. "Take it down a notch, buddy."

Chapman's voice was full of emotion. "You cannot shut me out of this. I've been waiting too long."

Rather than escalate the argument, Maginnis backed off. He needed time for Chapman to cool down. And he had to figure out how to handle him, after the file became an active case.

"Tell you what," he said. "I got some stuff to deal with right now. Why don't you come to my office this afternoon and we'll talk."

Maginnis read the agitation on Carter Chapman's face when the man appeared at his office door that afternoon. Chapman still looked like he was about to explode. Better tread softly.

Maginnis leaned back in his chair and grinned. "I gotta hand it to you, buddy. In my entire career, I've never seen a fish fly into the bucket this fast. I'm not gonna look a gift horse in the mouth. This is looking like a hum-dinger of a case."

"I'm beyond ready for it."

Maginnis raised a hand. "Hold on. You know I can't let you get involved. I'll be handling it from here."

He noticed a large vein pulsing in Chapman's neck. No way the guy was backing off.

"Tell you what," the agent conceded. "If there's some fancy cyber-sleuthing you want to do, I can probably let that happen."

Chapman looked grim. "I've done it. I just need to talk to her."

"Talk to her? You?"

"Yes."

Maginnis shook his head. "We've been over this, man. You're not a field agent. You're not even an office grunt, for Pete's sake. Let me be clear. You. Do. Not. Work. Here."

Chapman's glare held Maginnis in a death grip.

Maginnis tried again. "Look, it's great that you uncovered this one for us. You know how short-handed we are, with everything else going on in this crazy world. But I'm out on a limb as it is letting you near this case."

Chapman leaned over Maginnis's desk, his voice barely above a whisper. "This case is personal. It wouldn't even be on your radar if I hadn't laid it in your lap. You cannot take it away from me. You can't."

Maginnis eyed Chapman's clenched fists and softened his tone. "Buddy, you're a cyber-whiz, not an interrogator. What are you gonna do, try to charm the panties off the woman? Think that'll make her tell you everything you want to know? It's my butt on the line if you blow it."

Chapman leaned closer, his face only inches away from the agent's. "I wasn't always a computer nerd, my friend. You have no idea what I'm capable of. This is my life, and no bureaucratic baboon can tell me what I can and cannot do!"

Maginnis sprang from his chair and poked his finger hard into Chapman's chest. "Back off. Now. Before you do something stupid. You think you can march in here, raid our files and call the shots?"

Chapman grabbed Maginnis's wrist, twisted it and flung him back into his chair. The agent popped up again and raised a fist, ready to inflict damage. But before he could swing, Chapman backed away.

The agent lowered his fist. They exchanged sheepish looks.

"You're not keeping me out of this." Chapman's voice trembled with emotion. "I'm pursuing it, even if I have to work alone."

The agent smoothed the few strands left on top of his balding head. "I can take you down, you know."

"Not in this fight."

It was pointless to reignite the argument. As Chapman had described it, the case could be huge. A career-topper. This close to retirement, one more commendation wouldn't hurt. But still.

Maginnis shook his head. "You don't know anything about this woman, fella. How much she's involved, or anything."

"I know enough. More than you do, actually."

The agent lowered himself into his chair, still slightly breathless from the physical confrontation. "I'm beginning to regret that I didn't turn your butt in yesterday. It's only out of respect for your situation that I don't get you permanently exiled from these hallowed halls."

"I have to talk to this person myself," Chapman said. "Besides, I've already started."

"You . . . what?"

"I've been working on this a while, remember? It's what brought me here in the first place. I'm not looking for another contract with the FBI, or anybody else for that matter. I don't need the money. I have enough to last ten lifetimes. But I do need your cooperation. I won't let you down. I have a lot more at stake than you do."

Maginnis weighed the situation. Chapman had reams of data pointing to the likelihood that De Theret International was a player in more than one ongoing FBI investigation. And it was easy to sympathize with the guy's personal story. But allowing him to talk to a material witness, someone who could even be a potential suspect? That was too much.

And yet, if you were going to stick your neck out for someone, the odds favored Chapman. He was solid, no doubt, and motivated. Even if he was a royal pain in the backside.

Maginnis sighed. "Tell me how you want to handle it."

Chapman seemed to relax a bit. He sat across from the agent and outlined his plan.

Maginnis shook his head. "You know I could lose my job for this."

Chapman didn't budge.

The agent knew he might live to regret it, but if he were in Chapman's shoes, he'd want the same thing.

"Okay," he relented. "You can talk to her, but make it quick. It'll take a day or so to open an official file. After that, it's strictly FBI business. We'll do it my way from there on. Agreed?"

Chapman nodded.

"I mean it, buddy," Maginnis said. "You'll follow my lead. This will be my case, got it?"

"Got it."

"You don't make a move without me. Understand?"

Chapman nodded again.

"And if I ever hear anything like that 'baboon' garbage again, I'm gonna deck ya."

CHAPTER SIX

The Last Time

A couple of hours and my life will be my own again, Lista Pearson thought as she double-checked the text on her phone against the number on the hotel room door. Twelve thirty-two. This was it.

She noticed that Samantha had called again. Soon enough she'd be able to tell her what was going on. She'd written her a letter, but it was still in her purse. No point mailing it now, since she'd be leaving New Orleans and heading home today.

She dropped the phone into her purse, then took a minute to collect herself. She peeled the sodden jacket off her sweating frame and blotted her moist cheeks with the back of her hand.

She didn't have any regulars scheduled today, and when a new call came in, the idea of not showing up had briefly flickered in her mind. Hard, heavy rain threatened to shut down the streets, and there were more important things to get done before her flight left. But she'd quickly reconsidered.

It was the money, mostly, tons more than her personnel job at De Theret International paid. In less than two weeks, she'd nearly tripled her old monthly salary. Some men actually preferred bigger girls, especially redheads. That made up for a lot.

This was the last one, for sure. By the time anybody discovered that she had walked out with the entire thousand-dollar fee, she would be miles away. She wanted a real life in a real place where you didn't have to pretend you were somebody you weren't. She was going home to Nebraska.

Garbled television noises filtered through the door. It sounded like one of the skin flicks this otherwise elegant New Orleans hotel provided to its guests, for a fee.

The client had requested a big girl for a nooner, not all day. She'd have plenty of time to make her late afternoon flight. By sunset, she'd be home.

She knocked. The television noise stopped. The door opened, and Lista saw her client.

He was big, the largest man she'd ever seen. In her experience, it was mostly little guys who asked for big girls. This one looked like the giant at the top of Jack's beanstalk. She felt small as a sparrow.

"Mr. Burns?" It was the name all her clients were given. She sounded as tiny as she felt.

"You Bunny?" he growled.

She nodded.

"You're not fat enough."

"Are you Mr. Burns?" It was all she could think to say. Maybe she should have skipped out before this one.

"Yeah, if you say so." His eyes narrowed as he assessed her physical attributes. "You the biggest they got?"

She was speechless. Usually these clients told her how beautiful she was. They were gentlemen, really, mostly successful businessmen, or politicians with good manners, and polite, almost worshipful. That was the only pleasurable part of this latest mess she had gotten herself into. That, and the money.

He eyed her luggage. "What's in the case? Equipment?" He brightened, showing a row of uneven, yellowed teeth beneath his dark mustache.

"Sort of. It's mainly so I look like a regular hotel guest. But if you're disappointed, I can leave." *Say leave, say leave. Please.*

"So . . . what kind of equipment you got that you need such a big suitcase?" The smell of liquor from his breath oozed into the hallway.

"Look, if you want me to go, I will," she said. "I don't want to stand in the hall like this." She bent down to grab her jacket and purse.

"Come in."

She thought about the money. Only an hour. It won't be that bad. She walked in.

He shut the door behind her, threw the bolt, turned the latch and attached the chain guard.

His focus shifted back to the suitcase. "So, what's in the bag?" His tongue flicked rapidly across the dark fringe above his lips.

She took a deep, calming breath. In the sexy tone she'd practiced a hundred times in front of her mirror, she began her routine. "Why don't we get business out of the way so we can have our fun without any interruptions?"

She set the travel bag beside the wet bar. "You give me the money, and then you can tell me what you want." A chill coursed through her each time those words came out of her mouth.

He rubbed his beefy hands together. "Do I get to see what's in the bag?"

Her pulse quickened. There was nothing in the bag but the things she'd packed for the trip home: clothes, toiletries and a couple of files from her office at De Theret.

"You wouldn't like what's in it. It's not worth it, really."

"Why not?"

"They make me charge another five hundred for it. Personally, I think it's a waste. I promise we'll have a good time without it, just you and me."

He dug a small wad of hundred-dollar bills from his pants pocket, unfolded them, and counted. Not enough. A wave of relief washed over her.

She opened her purse to put the thousand inside and caught a glimpse of her plane ticket. Not much longer, and she'd be free. She just had to figure out how to get the client's focus away from her suitcase.

The man switched the television on again. The voices Lista had heard from the hallway now had faces and bodies. She'd seen this movie before, with another client.

He lurched across the room and sat on the king-sized bed, leering at her. "You shy or something? Strip! Let's see what I paid for."

She undressed slowly, draping each piece of clothing over a chair, until she peeled down to her two-piece red lace undies. She moved toward the bed and stood before him.

He x-rayed every inch of her body. She shivered, less from the temperature of the room than from the coldness of his stare.

"Turn around."

She circled in front of him slowly and came around to face him again. He pulled her closer with his massive hands. They felt like sandpaper. His breath reeked.

This guy was way too scary. Somehow, she had to take control. But first, she had to calm her racing pulse.

"Tell you what," she said. "I can tell you don't like me. I'll give you your money back. And I'll call the agency and tell them you want somebody bigger. I'm sure they'll send her over right away. Probably even give you a discount for your trouble. No harm done, okay?"

"I want what's in the case."

"But I told you—"

"For free. No extra five hundred."

"I can't do that. The agency—"

"Who's gonna tell 'em?" The veins in his neck bulged like jungle vines on a tree trunk. "Show me what's in the case!"

He crossed the room, grabbed the case and tried to open it. When the lock didn't budge, he banged the case against a chair. Again and again, he hefted the bag in the air and slammed it down, until the back of the chair cracked.

Another slam. The chair's back buckled against the seat and a leg splintered.

Lista's heart was pounding so hard, she nearly fainted. Without a thought for clothes, she grabbed her purse and ran to the door. Hands trembling, she worked the bolt, and then the latch. The door came open, but the safety chain caught it short.

She slammed the door and tried to work the chain out of its slot. Just as it fell free, she saw from the corner of her eye the airborne bulk of her suitcase, hurtling toward her.

CHAPTER SEVEN

Training Day

Gertie was waiting at the door to Samantha's office with a thumb drive in her hand. She handed it to Samantha.

"Here's your regular eight-thirty public image presentation for the new management trainees. It's eight-thirty now."

Training day. Samantha let out a groan.

At least the topic was one she knew by heart. The importance of fostering the company's positive public image had once been her favorite training topic. But her growing suspicions had dampened her enthusiasm for the subject.

Thumb drive in hand, she returned to the elevator, hoping the brief ride would give her enough time to summon a happy face.

She reached the tall double doors to the second-floor training room, took a deep breath, and walked in.

Kevin Molton turned from the blackboard where he had been scrawling an outline for the assembled class of twelve. "Ms. Newman! May I help you?"

"Yes, Kevin. I'm here to give my talk to the trainees today. Sorry I'm late."

Molton, the training coordinator for De Theret International, looked puzzled. "This morning?"

She nodded.

"But Ms. Odom told me to reschedule you. She was afraid you might be too tired after your trip. I'm doing Interview Follow-up this morning. Didn't you check the updates?" There was a hint of reproach in his voice.

It took no time for Samantha to recognize another one of E.B.'s slimy tricks. She squelched her first instinct, which was to roar invective at E.B. while strangling the life out of the she-wolf's uptight acolyte, Kevin Molton.

"No, it's Ms. Odom who has—" She caught herself, checked her tone, and continued. "Actually, I'm glad for the unscheduled time. I have too much work as it is today. Hope to see you all again soon." She put on a bright smile, made her exit and steamed toward the elevator.

On her way back up to the executive floor, she came to a decision.

This is where it stops, Eula Beth.

Samantha swung by her office and dropped the thumb drive on Gertie's desk. She turned to leave again. "I'll be in E.B.'s office for a few minutes."

"E.B.'s office?" Gertie knew her boss avoided E.B. Odom whenever possible, and there was no meeting between them on the morning schedule.

"Yes, E.B.'s office. There's unfinished business to take care of. Shouldn't take long."

"Okay," the baffled assistant replied as her boss disappeared out the door.

Without stopping to let E.B.'s assistant announce her visit, Samantha marched past the door to her private office and strode up to the desk.

"I'm sure I'm not interrupting anything important. Am I?"

E.B. was studying her reflection in a hand mirror. She had barely looked up when Samantha entered.

Despite the woman's feigned indifference, Samantha knew that E.B.'s radar was on alert. She leaned over the desk until she was practically in her face.

"I have some news for you, Eula Beth." She purposely used the woman's real name to annoy her. "I am through with your stupid games and your little intrigues. And more importantly, you are through with them. It all stops now."

E.B. applied a fresh smear of lip gloss and checked the mirror again. "I can't imagine what you're talking about, Samantha. Are you feeling okay? Maybe you should sit down."

Samantha laughed. "You've never been concerned about another human being in your life, least of all me. But you're not going to get your claws in my business anymore. I've had it with your underhanded behavior. It's over, understand?"

E.B. returned the gloss to a desk drawer. "This is about Derek, isn't it? You still want him. You kicked him out, and now you want him back. Not that I blame you. He's one sexy man. Too bad he's found another playmate. One that suits him just fine."

Samantha wanted to scream. She fought for control and lowered her voice.

"This has nothing to do with Derek. He's free to do what he wants. But he's way too smart for your little tricks, so I'd suggest you find another toy. I'm sure you have plenty of candidates lined up."

"I'm afraid you're wrong. Derek and I, we're . . . we're working closely together, him and me, and—"

"Have it your way. I'm sure Vinson won't mind that he's sharing you with Derek."

E.B.'s smile vanished. "You wouldn't dare. Besides, he won't believe you."

"That's where *you're* wrong, Eula Beth. I may not have the same kind of influence over him, but Vinson knows that I speak the truth. He'll believe me, and you know it."

"But—"

"Don't risk it. I'm warning you."

With E.B.'s silence, Samantha knew she had struck a blow. Emboldened, she continued.

"So here's what's going to happen, Ms. Odom. You will stop undermining my job. Any feeling I get that you're playing your games again, I'll go straight to Vinson with news about your latest boy-toy. And I'll add the names of the others you've been with since Trey disappeared."

The last detail was only conjecture on Samantha's part, but by the look on E.B.'s face, the threat had hit home. For once, the woman looked wilted.

"You may return to your very important work now." Samantha started to leave, then stopped at the door and delivered one last volley.

"By the way, I think I saw a zit on your chin. Have a nice day."

CHAPTER EIGHT

Network News

Fresh from her confrontation with E.B., Samantha was exhilarated.

She was still cooling down when Gertie buzzed. "Some guy from the News Journal Reports TV show is on line one."

"News Journal Reports? I wonder what they want." She picked up the receiver.

"Samantha Newman."

"Ms. Newman, my name is Roland Dabney." The man's voice carried a distinctly adenoidal New York accent. "I'm a producer for News Journal Reports. You are familiar with the show?"

"Of course." Everyone knew News Journal Reports, the popular weekly show that featured human interest and news stories generously peppered with investigative reports. "What can I do for you, Mr. Dabney?"

"We did a show a few years back on the migration of the labor force from the traditional industrial communities in the Northeast to the growing opportunities in the South. Kind of a Rust Belt to Sun Belt thing. You might have seen it?"

"I did. Very interesting."

"Thanks," Dabney said. "We're working on a follow-up, revisiting the idea with a piece that features people in Houston. I understand that you're the person who handles media inquiries at your company."

"I am. Exactly what are you interested in?"

"We're comparing the situations people left back East to the kind of life they have now. We've already got two people, but we need one more for balance: a high-level executive who left a cushy job up north and gambled on a new career in the South. We're having a little difficulty finding the right person. I understand your company is a strong player in the Houston market, so we wondered if you might have a client who fits the profile and who would be willing to talk to us."

Samantha sat up. It would be a feather in her cap to get De Theret International mentioned favorably on a top prime time news show. It could keep her in Vinson's good graces for a while longer. "I'm sure we can provide you with several likely candidates. How soon do you—"

"Anyway," Dabney's voice cut in. "I'm going to be in Houston tomorrow. Can we meet for an early lunch, say, eleven-thirty at my hotel? It's The Lancaster. Do you know it?"

"Yes." He certainly was getting right to the point. Maybe he was rushed for time.

"Good. Sorry for the short notice. See you then."

"Shall I—?"

He hung up before she had a chance to ask how she would recognize him. "See you then," she said to the dial tone.

She pressed the intercom button. "Get Derek on the line, please, Gertie."

No matter how awkward it was, it was impossible to avoid Derek at work. And now, he was the one she needed to help her with candidates for the News Journal Reports piece. The files in his Executives International division were full of likely possibilities.

As she waited for him to come on the line, her mind replayed the smackdown with E.B. She wished she could tell Lista about it. But there was still no word from her, or from the FBI, for that matter.

Gertie's voice broke in. "Derek, line two."

Samantha hit the speaker button, determined to make the conversation brief.

"I need a body."

"But the one you have is perfect."

She could almost see him grinning. She replied with stony silence.

"Sorry." He cleared his throat. "What can I do for you, Ms. Newman?"

"I'm looking for a former Rust Belt executive."

"Didn't know you had a thing for Yankees."

Again, she ignored the joke. "I need to look at the files of the ones we've placed, especially those who had decent jobs back East but who found even better situations through us. It's kind of a rush. By end of day, if you can."

"Your command is my wish, sweetheart. I count the hours."

Samantha disconnected. Her mind traveled back to the good times she and Derek once shared, and the thrill she used to feel whenever she scored a big PR coup for De Theret like this new one promised to be.

Everything good in her life had soured. She needed to move on. To find joy again. But not until after she found Lista.

CHAPTER NINE

Play-Act

The Lancaster Hotel nestled among the towering skyscrapers of downtown Houston, a gem of an inn in the performing arts district. Flanked by The Alley, a repertory theater, to the west and Jones Hall, a cavernous concert venue to the south, it had survived various swings of fortune in its nearly hundred-year history.

Briefcase in hand, Samantha strode through the entrance. She paused in the foyer and scanned the lobby for anyone who could be Roland Dabney. One man occupied a cozy sitting area. Although he was obscured by the newspaper he was reading, he didn't match her image of the person she had spoken to yesterday.

She spotted a house phone nearby. As she took the receiver from its cradle, she noticed the man with the newspaper staring at her.

It couldn't be Roland Dabney. This man was more a news anchor type than a behind-the-scenes producer, and twice as good-looking as she expected him to be.

She could feel his eyes on her as she waited for an operator to answer. A thrill ran through her. Too bad he wasn't waiting for her.

"Roland Dabney's room, please," she said when the operator answered.

"Ms. Newman?"

She turned. The man with the newspaper rose and spoke again.

"Are you Samantha Newman?"

She lowered the receiver. "Roland Dabney?"

She still doubted that this could be the person she spoke to yesterday. His voice was deeper, more assured and controlled than Dabney's, and there was no hint of a New York accent in this man's easy drawl.

"No." The man smiled. His warm brown eyes held her in his gaze. "Mr. Dabney didn't make the trip. I'm here in his place. Sorry for the last-minute switch."

"No need to apologize." She fought to control a grin before it spread ear to ear and offered her hand. "Samantha Newman."

"Carter Chapman." He took her hand in his. It felt warm and strong and . . . comfortable. She was grateful to Dabney for not showing up.

"Ready for lunch?" Chapman asked. "I think our table is waiting."

In the small, sleek restaurant, only a few steps across the lobby, they were seated by a window with a street-level view of the city's lunchtime bustle. Several cars slowed as they neared the hotel's valet stand. Soon the restaurant would fill to capacity.

Samantha set her briefcase under the table. "I brought resumes of a few executives you might be interested in."

"Maybe later," Chapman said. "For now, let's start with your company. I'd like to know more about it."

The good news or the bad? She could recite the usual PR blah-blah in her sleep. But there was something about the man sitting across from her. Something genuine. Odd, to feel so comfortable with him at the outset, especially since she had stopped trusting almost everyone she knew. But this was a business lunch, and the PR talk was mandatory.

"What do you want to know?"

"First, I'd like to know if you want a cocktail."

She declined. It would be hard enough to keep her wits about her.

"Then let's take a minute to order, get that out of the way so we can talk."

He certainly knew how to take charge of an interview. She scanned the menu and chose the ahi tuna.

"Steak salad for me." Chapman handed their menus to the waiter. "Wine?"

She shook her head.

With the waiter out of the way, Chapman leaned in. "Now we can talk about you."

"You mean my company?"

A nod confirmed it.

She began the way she always did when reciting the success story of De Theret International.

"About a decade ago, Vinson De Theret was managing a small employment agency. A big headache for him was finding qualified assistants for the top-level executives. Most agencies offered under-qualified people, which was a waste of everybody's time. De Theret began to train his own candidates, making sure that they excelled in all the administrative skills, and that they looked and acted like professionals capable of doing anything they were asked to do."

"Anything?"

The question threw her. What was he suggesting? His face gave no clue.

"Anything a competent executive assistant should be doing."

The answer seemed to satisfy him, so she continued. "De Theret quit his job and opened Elite Professionals, the agency that became the cornerstone of De Theret International. In less than two years, it was the largest and most successful placement agency in the city."

She usually paused at this point to let the interviewer ask questions, but Chapman seemed content to listen, so she continued on about the rapid growth of De Theret agencies around the country, their expansion into executive search, and their peripheral services like the project management work in South America.

"In just a few years, De Theret International became a powerhouse in the human resources industry, nationally and internationally."

The waiter brought bread to the table and promised to return with their food. She was glad for an excuse to stop talking. It both surprised and disgusted her that she could still sound so enthusiastic about her employer.

Chapman had not taken his eyes off her during her dissertation. "I am amazed."

"At what?"

"At you."

"Me?" Heat rose in her cheeks. Was he flirting?

His eyes were still locked on her. "I'm amazed at how well you do your job. Despite your feelings."

Feelings? How did he know what she felt? And what did that have to do with the News Journal Reports story?

"I don't understand what you mean."

"Your message led me to believe . . ."

Message? She hadn't sent this man a message. She hadn't sent one to Roland Dabney either. What was he talking about?

He lowered his voice. "You have serious concerns about your company, do you not?"

Concerns? How did he know?

A wave of nausea gripped her. She grabbed her water glass to take a sip. It shook in her hand. She set it down and hid both hands in her lap.

Chapman leaned in. "You are missing a person, I believe, by the name of Lista Pearson?"

She struggled to respond, but no words came.

He softened his tone. "I didn't mean to alarm you, Ms. Newman. I know you expected to meet with someone from News Journal Reports. Apologies, but the call was a subterfuge. I'm actually here in response to the message you sent to—"

"—the FBI?"

He nodded.

Why hadn't he told her who he was from the beginning, instead of leading her through that disgusting charade?

Her mind was spinning. For months, she'd carefully hidden her true feelings about De Theret International. Now that the secret fears she'd shared with no one were exposed, she wanted to take them back. She wished she had never sent that message. But it was too late.

Her heart raced. She was deeply embarrassed by the corporate blather she'd spouted to the man across from her. But more than that, she was furious.

She pushed away from the table. "What kind of game is this?"

A few diners looked up from their lunch to stare. She lowered her voice, but it was hard to control the rage.

"Do you get your kicks by making fools out of people?"

Blood rushed to her face again. She shut her eyes tight to stop the hot tears that brimmed to overflowing. The cool, levelheaded business persona she had carefully cultivated for years had all but vanished. She was frightened and flustered and ashamed and angry, and she was about to come undone, right there in the restaurant.

A strong hand grasped hers. "I'm sorry. I didn't mean to . . ."

Risking tears, she opened her eyes. Chapman's face swam before her in a watery blur. Something in his voice and the warmth of his hand slowed her panic, but her heart was still sprinting.

The urge to flee was strong. She extracted her hand, and without another word, she stood and sped to the ladies' room.

When she reached the marbled coolness of the powder room, she was grateful to find it empty. She yanked a tissue from the box on the countertop and faced the mirror, prepared to see her reflected self crumble into miserable sobs.

But instead of her pitiful reflection, she was shocked to see a well-composed face staring back at her in bewilderment. She tried to screw her muscles into crying mode, but tears wouldn't come. She blotted her eyes, still moist from the initial panic, and waited.

Calm settled over her. She stuck her tongue out and watched the reflection mock her. Then she began to laugh.

She didn't know what to make of the situation, or of her odd reaction to it. Maybe now that her secret fears were out in the world, the pressure she'd been living under was relieved. Or maybe it was Carter Chapman—if that was his real name—and his ridiculous, stupid ploy.

It made her smile to think of him, sitting alone in the restaurant, probably flustered by his mishandling of the interrogation, or whatever it was supposed to have been. Served him right for trying such a dumb, manipulative stunt. Why hadn't he just come out and told her who he was to begin with?

She dawdled in the powder room's sweet-scented solitude. For all the discomfort Chapman had put her through, she felt a tingle of excitement.

How could a stranger push her to the brink of so many feelings in the first few minutes of their meeting? He didn't strike her as the gray, faceless bureaucrat he now claimed to be.

There was a knock on the powder room door.

"Ms. Newman?" a man's muffled voice called. The door pushed open a crack. Chapman.

She yanked the door fully open and glared. "What is it? Not finished humiliating me yet?"

"I brought your purse, in case you needed to freshen up or something."

"Did you conduct a thorough FBI search of it?" She didn't bother to hide the sarcasm.

"No."

His face held a look of regret. But she was not about to let him off easy. She yanked the bag out of his hand.

"I suppose you're accustomed to reducing your victims to giant puddles of tears, Mr. Carter, or Chapman, or whoever you are. However, I'm fine. Sorry to disappoint you."

She brushed past him and headed toward the restaurant. He followed, half running to keep up. She quickened her pace to stay ahead of him.

He caught up to her at their table. "You are the last person I'd want to find in a giant puddle. I'd really like to start over. Do you think we could continue with lunch?"

"I've enjoyed all the lunch I can stand for one day." She stooped to retrieve her briefcase. "It's been swell meeting you and seeing how seriously my government's servants take their jobs. Goodbye."

She strode away through the door to the street.

Chapman quickly settled the check and followed her to the valet stand. "I'll just wait with you until they bring your car."

He looked downright abashed. "I am truly sorry, Ms. Newman. I'd planned to tell you who I was right away, but, when I met you . . . I don't know, I just wanted to . . ." He stopped and looked away. Despite his self-assured manner, there was something sad about him.

The valet returned with Samantha's ticket and car keys. "Ma'am," he said, "your car don't want to start."

"Oh, great." She loved her car, but it had been a little flaky for months. This was no time for it to fail her, again.

"Let me try it," Chapman suggested. "I'm pretty good with cars." He seemed eager to redeem himself.

"No need. I'm sure it's the same mystery ailment the garage has been struggling with for a while. I'll call and tell them to come get it. They're used to it by now."

"Then I will drive you back to your office," he offered. "Or wherever you want to go."

"No thanks."

"I insist." He handed his ticket to the valet. "You can call the repair shop while they bring my car around. Really, I'd like a chance to show you that I'm not a complete jackass. I'm really kind of a good guy, actually. I don't know what I was thinking back there."

Samantha considered her options. Chapman seemed genuinely sorry. And there was something else about him she couldn't quite put a finger on, something trustworthy, despite his ridiculous deception.

"Okay." She pulled her cell phone from her purse and called the repair shop. The street noise made it difficult to hear, so she reentered the lobby to talk. She ended the call and returned to the street.

A Rolls Royce Silver Cloud sat at the curb in front of her, with Chapman at the wheel. Once again, the guy had produced a bombshell. The valet held the passenger door open for her.

She slid into the cushy seat and took in the car's leathery scent. "You are full of surprises. Or is this Roland Dabney's car?"

"No, this is Carter Chapman's car," he said. "And I *am* Carter Chapman."

"Is this what the FBI issues its agents these days? My tax dollars at work."

He smiled as he pulled away from the curb. "No, this is my personal car. I, uh . . . I don't really work for the FBI."

So much for trustworthy. She reached for the door handle. "Stop the car, please. I'm getting out."

"No, wait," he pleaded. "Let me explain. I work *with* the FBI, as an independent contractor."

She kept her grip on the handle. "Do you just make stuff up as you go along and wait for something to stick? I'm not interested in hearing more lies, Mr. Chapman. Let me out now!"

He pulled the car to the curb and unlocked the door. She opened it to leave, but before she could unbuckle the seatbelt, his hand gently touched her elbow.

"Please, I'm telling the truth, I swear. Let me explain."

She let go of the buckle.

"I'm not a liar," he said. "Despite my ineptitude today, I haven't lied to you once. I told you that I'm working with the FBI, and that's the truth."

There were those eyes again. She wavered. "So, your name really is Carter Chapman?"

"Yes."

"And you work with the FBI?"

"I've been a consultant for them for years now. Mostly in cyber-crimes, but—"

"Cybercrimes? What's that got to do with me?"

"It's a long story."

"Never mind. I'm not up to any more stories today." She pulled the door shut. "Just take me to my office, please."

He looked relieved as he steered the Rolls smoothly into the flow of traffic again.

"This really is your car?"

"Yes, though I rarely drive it. But it's been needing some exercise."

"So, where's your chauffeur?"

"His day off. Actually, he seldom drives for me. Mostly he just takes care of the cars and helps me manage work at the ranch."

The ranch? A chauffeur, a Rolls Royce, and . . . a ranch? Had she fallen down a Texas-sized jackrabbit hole?

She studied Chapman's strong profile. Somehow, it wasn't that hard to believe the extraordinary things he was saying. She had a feeling he was not in the habit of lying, even though he had tried to deceive her. After all, he'd handled that like an amateur.

He turned onto Allen Parkway. The day was cooler than normal, and bright sunshine had encouraged more than the usual number of downtown office workers to take an outdoor lunch break. Some people relaxed on benches, while others in jogging attire skittered along the running path in at the edge of Buffalo Bayou.

A mile or two later, Carter broke the silence that had descended. "Do you think we could continue, or maybe start over with our conversation?"

"Not today. Sorry."

"Please, don't apologize." He reached over and put his warm, strong hand on hers. "This whole thing was my fault. I have no idea why I . . . I'm usually not . . . It's just that, I . . . well, I hope you know how sorry I am that I upset you."

The Rolls came to a stop at the entrance to the De Theret International building. Chapman cut the engine and turned to face her. "Before you go, I want to say something."

"Not necessary." She was poised to open the door and flee, but part of her wanted to hear what he had to say. She took her hand off the door release and turned to him. "Okay, speak."

"My name really is Carter Chapman. I really do work with the FBI, as a consultant. This really is my car. Most of the year, I live on my ranch and commute by helicopter or plane, depending on where my client is. On days like this, I drive myself.

"I hope you don't take all this for bragging," he continued. "I certainly don't mean it to be. It's simply the truth. I'm not usually the jerk I was with you today. I hope very much that you'll forgive me."

Those sad eyes again.

She softened. "Forget it. I probably overreacted. I've been under a lot of stress lately. Everybody has problems. I don't want to burden you with mine."

She didn't know if she meant what she was saying, but now that the FBI had responded, albeit in this unexpected way, she needed more time to think.

Maybe her instincts were wrong about De Theret. Maybe she was merely reacting to her personal job frustrations. Companies were like people, with their own idiosyncrasies. God knows De Theret had a few of those. And Lista . . . maybe Derek was right, and her friend was away on one of her crazy escapades.

"I cannot forget it, Ms. Newman," Chapman said.

"Why not?"

"Two reasons. First, because your suspicions about De Theret align with bits of information I've been gathering for an investigation of my own. Helping you find your friend may lead to the piece of the puzzle I need to complete that picture.

"My original intention was to extract as much information as I could from you, without disclosing the full scope of my investigation. That's why I tried to play that stupid game with you. But I found it difficult to be less than honest with you. You're not exactly what I expected. I'm sorry for treating you so badly."

"I'm fine, Mr. Chapman. Really."

She offered a smile. He returned one of his own. It melted any resolve she had to end the conversation.

"So, what exactly is 'the full scope' of your investigation?" She wasn't sure she was ready to hear the answer. Was he saying that her fears were well-founded after all?

"Sorry. I can't discuss it with you yet. I know that sounds lousy in view of what I just said, but it's important that you be debriefed first, before we contaminate what you know with our own information. Does that make sense?"

She considered what he'd said. "I suppose it does. But you mentioned two reasons why you didn't want to forget this whole thing. What's the other one?"

He studied her a long time before he answered. "It may not be appropriate to say this, but I can't help it. I want to see you again, for personal reasons. I want to start over on the right foot. You don't deserve what I did to you today."

"Forget it."

"I told you, I cannot just forget it. I suspect that De Theret International is in the middle of some ugly things, and you're in the middle of De Theret. I don't mean to make it sound like you're Little Red Riding Hood and need to be protected from the big, bad wolf, but that could very well be the case."

A familiar tickle of dread caught in her throat. The mix of emotions that had swirled through her at their lunch meeting had taken a toll. She couldn't bear to hear any more.

"I can take care of myself." She opened the door to get out.

"Just think about everything I've said," he pleaded. "I know you will. When you're ready, call me. Please. Here is my card."

She took the card and put it in her pocket. "Thanks for the buggy ride. And don't be so hard on yourself. At least it wasn't another boring business lunch." She gave Chapman a wry smile and stepped out. As she turned to enter the building, she almost tripped over E.B. Odom.

E.B.'s eyes traveled from the Rolls, to Chapman, to Samantha and back to the car.

Samantha didn't stop to acknowledge her presence. But she did notice the play of shock, jealousy and anger on the woman's face. It was naive to believe that their battle was over, but for now, Samantha shrugged it off.

More pressing problems crowded her mind. Chapman's warning lingered as she made her way inside. Were the ugly things he referred to the same ones that worried her? Or could they be worse than she imagined?

CHAPTER TEN

A Teensy Favor

After her unsettling meeting with Carter Chapman, Samantha tried to focus on the piles of work covering her desk, among them, proofs of promotional material awaiting her approval and a tower of reports.

She pushed the quarterly printouts to the farthest corner. They hadn't reflected reality for some time, anyway.

Attending to the new promotion schedule was even harder. There was no use to even try to conjure up enthusiasm for it.

Lazy wasn't the word for what she felt. Paralyzed was more like it.

It was her own fault. Why was she the one who couldn't accept the status quo, the questioner, the stupid fool for asking? Where had it gotten her?

Maybe she was being too hard on herself. The split with Derek had nearly ripped her apart. She ached for the old days, when his reassuring presence could steady her rocky world. But those days were gone for good.

She missed Lista, too. True, her old college roommate had a penchant for getting into foolish trouble that stuck with her through the years. A stream of parking tickets, an occasionally overdrawn bank account, a slew of bad boyfriends. But Lista was a caring person, and the only one in Samantha's life, besides Derek, who shared a history. And she owed her so much.

She couldn't stop thinking about Carter Chapman. Never had she met someone she was so instantly comfortable with, despite the circumstances. Was she really so lonely that she could be attracted to a guy who'd behaved like a complete jerk?

His card was still in her pocket. Less than an hour ago he'd confirmed that something serious was going on within De Theret. If Lista really was in jeopardy, and Chapman could help find her, Samantha had to follow through and finish what she'd started.

She pulled the card out and looked at it for the first time. It carried no FBI insignia, no job title, no address. Engraved in simple black print on thick buttery paper, it offered only his name and contact information.

Samantha sensed the presence of another person in her office. She looked up to see E.B. Odom smiling from the doorway.

"It's just little ol' me," E.B. giggled. "Your assistant isn't at her desk, so I just invited myself in. Didn't mean to scare you."

She shut the door and crossed to Samantha's desk where she perched, one leg up, on the corner. "I wonder if I might ask a teensy favor."

Samantha returned the card to her pocket and braced against the onslaught of E.B.'s perfume. "What is it?"

"I'm having a little problem with my Lexus, and I wondered if you might give me the name of your repair shop."

So, they were playing nice again. *As if.*

"Barney's, on Pine Street."

"Thanks. I'll give them a call."

E.B. didn't seem ready to leave. She riffled the stack of reports with her blood-red fingernails. The diamond in the nail of her index finger glinted in the late afternoon sunlight streaming through the window. She giggled again.

The hairs at the back of Samantha's neck prickled.

"By the way," E.B. cooed, "I couldn't help but notice the good-looking man in the gorgeous Rolls Royce who dropped you off today. A new boyfriend?"

"No."

"A client of ours?"

"Sort of." She could have easily said that the man was Roland Dabney from News Journal Reports and kept up the charade that Chapman had started. But that would encourage more questions than Samantha cared to answer.

What *had* happened to Roland Dabney, the person she was supposed to have met for lunch today? Chapman could answer that question, too. At any rate, it was nobody's business who the man in the Rolls was.

E.B. was not put off. "Well, if he is a new boyfriend, I congratulate you on your good taste." She paused to contemplate her manicure. "Who is he, really?"

"It was a business lunch, Eula Beth. To discuss some executives that he may want to interview. I really don't want to talk about it until I'm sure he's interested."

E.B. frowned. "Keeping secrets isn't good company policy, Samantha. If it's body business, I should meet him. You stick to getting us good PR, and the rest of us will do the real work."

Samantha chose not to take the bait. It was wasted breath, anyway. "There's no search fee here. Besides, it's not a secret. Derek gave me the resumes. I just don't want to make a big deal of it until I know if it's something."

She rose and walked to the door, hoping E.B. would recognize that the conversation was over.

E.B. remained on her perch. "Derek knows about it? I thought you two were no longer collaborating."

"It's our business. Derek, you, me. We all work together here, remember? And speaking of work, I have to get back to mine. Time for you to go."

E.B. took her time as she sauntered to the door. She paused at the threshold.

"One more thing, Samantha. Vinnie and I have noticed that you seem totally stressed lately. We're worried that the job might be too much for you.

Maybe you need a rest. A long vacation. It could be healthy for you."

Samantha smiled. "Gee, we could plan a trip together. Just the three of us. Wouldn't that be fun?"

E.B. looked confused. "Well, I don't think. . . I mean, I'm not sure . . ."

"Kidding, E.B. I'm kidding. Have a good day."

She shut the door tight as soon as the snake had slithered out.

CHAPTER ELEVEN

Printout

Maginnis's blood pressure skyrocketed. "What do you mean, *we* blew it?"

He paced behind his desk, red-faced and steaming. "I don't remember as how I was there at the time, which I shoulda been, you stupid sonafagun. Geez, man, I thought you had more sense than to—"

Chapman bore the tongue-lashing quietly. "*I* blew it. I blew it. All by myself."

"You? Mr. Suave? Mr. 'Retired to My Ranch at Thirty-three'? I didn't think you were capable of making a mistake."

He punched his chair, sending it into a spin. "My job, my career, thirty friggin' years! I never should have let you talk me into interrogating a witness. She was obviously too tough for a desk squatter like you."

"It wasn't that she was tough."

"What would you call it, then?"

Chapman loosened his tie. "Well, she wasn't nearly as . . . as. . . She was just different, somehow. Much less . . . much more . . ."

"Much less, much more," Maginnis echoed in a pinched singsong. "What the heck are you trying to say?"

Chapman started over. "I mean . . . I spent hours collecting and studying information on her. There's some interesting stuff there. I thought I had a pretty good feel for how to approach her. But she . . . she . . ."

"Threw you for a loop?" Maginnis offered.

Chapman covered his face with his hands. "I've probably blown the whole case. I should have listened to you. I blew it for both of us."

Maginnis returned to his desk to contemplate the situation. The screw-up had cost Chapman too. No use crucifying him, even if he deserved it.

"It was a dumb idea to start with," Maginnis admitted. "But with your pretty-boy charm, I thought your little charade might work. An old horse like me could never get away with it, but I figured it'd be fun to watch you try. My call, my fault. But if the lady really wants to find her friend, she'll come around, once she's had a chance to cool down. In the meantime, there are plenty of other angles to pursue."

Chapman rubbed his eyes. "I know. But I really thought she'd be the answer. I still think she's an important key. If there was some way I could get her to talk to me again, I . . . she . . . well, she's not . . . what I expected."

Maginnis slapped his desk. "Let it go, fella! You sound obsessed with her. She must be a looker."

Chapman reddened.

"Aha!" Maginnis crowed. "Am I a great investigator, or what? You've got the hots for our key witness!"

"Absolutely not!"

Maginnis grinned. "It happens. Even you are a human being, my man."

"Thanks for the compliment."

"De nada."

"And thanks for not sticking your fist through my skull, like I probably deserve."

Maginnis leaned back in his chair and propped his feet on the desk. "I try to avoid violence in my own office. Hate the cleanup after. But this is now an official case, and you are officially out of here."

"But—"

"Out. Of. Here."

"What if I—"

"What if you let me do the work I'm paid to do? I'm pretty good at it, by the way. Or do you want to duke it out again?" Maginnis stood, ready for a repeat of their last encounter.

"I was only going to say that I could still do the background work, keep up with all the loose ends for you. I can't drop this now, Mack. I won't drop it."

Chapman was harder to get rid of than pinkeye. Despite the risk, Maginnis didn't have the heart to turn him away.

"Well. . . your snazzy software has helped us solve some knotty cases. I'll give you that." He rubbed the fuzz of his bald spot. "What the hay, I suppose we still owe you. And I could use the help. But this can't go on forever."

He lifted a sheaf of papers from the desk. "These are the latest printouts from your convergence program."

Chapman took the papers. "Anything in here?"

Maginnis shook his head. "Haven't had time to check. Since you're still here, look 'em over. Report anything relevant to me. Then leave, and don't come back unless I call you."

Chapman eagerly rifled through the pages. "Thanks for this, Mack. I—"

"No speeches. Just take a look and go. I'm off to another headache." At the door, Maginnis paused. "I mean it, man. Look, report, and leave. Got it?"

Chapman nodded and walked out, his focus already on the printouts in his hand.

Maginnis shut the door behind him and returned to the other unsolved cases on his desk that needed his attention. Yet none seemed as intriguing as the one Carter Chapman had tipped him to. He shook his head. If Chapman discovered a new thread in those printouts, there was no way the guy would back off.

Down the hall, in the cubicle he'd set up for himself, Chapman eagerly scanned the day's reports. He quickly found the last section, where random unsolved incidents were listed by region. He pored over each entry, hoping to find one that might relate to the De Theret case.

His eyes caught on an entry.

He removed his suit jacket and read it again. His heart beat faster.

He gave the item another review, then picked up the phone and called the New Orleans bureau. Maybe luck was on his side, after all.

CHAPTER TWELVE

Carless

By week's end, Samantha couldn't shake the feeling that things were coming to a close for her at De Theret International.

Normally, she'd be in the thick of things, sitting in meetings with Vinson, advising him on almost every move he made, discussing how his future plans would impact the public image of the company.

But he hadn't invited her to his office in weeks, not since the last time, when they had clashed over Lista. It wouldn't be a shock if he fired her soon.

Once upon a time, her career meant everything to her. Still did, though she'd come to loathe the things she'd loved most about the job. Now, she only stuck around in hopes of finding Lista. After that, the future was a big blank.

She slogged through the correspondence and memos in front of her, making comments in the margins for Gertie to deal with next week.

The whiff of E.B.'s last visit to her office lingered. Why had she come, really? Certainly not to make friends. And what was all that fake concern over Samantha's wellbeing? In retrospect, it seemed like it might have been a threat.

She shook off the memory and started whittling down the list of phone messages. Halfway through. her intercom buzzed.

Gertie's voice came through. "Bad news. The garage called. Your car won't be ready until Monday."

"Monday? Great. I'm stranded over the weekend. How could Barney do this to me?"

"Maybe you should ask him. It was another mechanic who called. Apparently, they need a part that won't be in until Monday. Maybe they can give you a loaner. Want me to get Barney on the phone?"

Samantha checked the time. "Too late. They're already closed. Can you give me a lift home?"

"Sure," Gertie replied. "But I'm leaving soon. It's Friday night."

"Your Sabbath dinner. I still remember how lovely it was the time I was there."

"Why don't you come tonight?"

"Thanks, but not tonight. Rain check?"

"Of course," Gertie replied. "Oh, hold on . . . a call's coming in."

The phone went silent, then Gertie returned. "Derek on three."

"Hiya gorgeous!" His voice was full of enthusiasm.

"Hello, Derek."

"You sound kinda down for a Friday. Like your best friend just died."

"Just my car."

"Is it terminal this time?"

"I don't think so, but it'll be in the shop over the weekend."

"Bummer. Hey, I've got a great idea! I need to celebrate some good news with somebody who appreciates how good I am at this business. How about dinner at Nino's tonight?"

She met his offer with silence.

"Just dinner, I swear."

He wasn't playing fair. Nino's was one of her favorites. She ran through a half dozen reasons no to go. But without a car, the long weekend stretch looked bleak.

"Just dinner?"

"No funny business, I promise."

"Okay. Nino's sounds great."

"Super. Pick you up at seven-thirty."

As soon as they disconnected, Samantha regretted accepting Derek's invitation. She knew she'd be facing another round of mixed emotions. On the other hand, he could still make her feel cared for, and she longed for some of that again. He was in his usual high spirits, and she needed to be where good vibes were happening. Maybe it would rub off on her.

Or, depending on the news he wanted to share, it could end badly. Why hadn't she just said no?

CHAPTER THIRTEEN

Bad Boy

A humid, Gulf-driven fog shrouded the city. Heavy ground-hugging clouds had descended upon the glittery black carapace of the De Theret International Building, transforming its interior into an insular mirror-box. Each room, each desk, was reflected in every window.

Vinson De Theret loved the phenomenon. Weather like this brought to life the cherished vision in his mind's eye: endless acres of offices filled with desks and phone banks and client files. The hundreds of De Theret employees on every floor became nearly a thousand, all scurrying to serve multiplied clients for exponentially increased profits.

From the window of his cavernous private office, he gazed beyond his own reflection to the trappings within. His hand caressed the suede-upholstered wall as he inventoried the mirrored furnishings.

The desk, a trapezoid of gleaming rosewood, spread its broad back to the window. Beyond lay a vast expanse of sculpted mauve carpet that extended twenty feet to the door. At the center was a plush purple medallion that boldly displayed the logo of De Theret International.

This foggy evening, his milky blue, bloodshot eyes traveled to the other side of the room, where E.B.

Odom lounged on a sleek leather sofa, sipping bourbon as she watched the business news on a big screen.

De Theret's thumb rubbed at the suede as he took in the sight of her. Among all his possessions, she was his most precious. Without her, his profits—and his pleasures—would be diminished by half. His heart swelled to look at her.

She called to him from across the room. "Did you hear what I said, Vinnie?"

He turned away from the window. "No, I didn't, darling. I was thinking about how much you mean to me."

"That's nice." She pushed a button on the remote, and the screen went silent. "But I want you to listen to me. That goody-two-shoes is gonna cause trouble for us one day."

She stirred the ice in her glass with her diamond-studded fingernail and licked the boozy liquid from her finger.

"Let's not fight about this again, please. We need her."

He joined E.B. on the sofa. "Samantha built our public image. She's classy. She helped move us from a two-bit employment agency to a top-tier player. All that great PR she gets for us. You know how most people think of us in the body business, and she—"

"Aren't I classy, Vinnie?"

"Of course you are, darling. The classiest."

"Then we don't need her anymore, do we?"

De Theret frowned. "Please don't ask me to fire her. I know she's been a pain lately, but she means too much to the company."

Arguing with E.B. always made him anxious. He struggled to head off a round of facial tics.

Craving relief, he took her hand and traced a line with her sharp fingernails across the inside of his freckled wrist, one nail at a time, pressing harder with each finger.

He imagined being stroked by a wild tiger. Crimson streaks rose on his pale skin. His blinking slowed.

E.B. ignored his attempt to distract her. "She doesn't respect me like she should, Vinnie. Thinks she's better than me. She's liable to be trouble one day. Get rid of her, now. I mean it. And stop that! You'll break a nail."

He let go and stared at the red welts on his wrist.

A buzz erupted from E.B.'s bosom: her cell phone. She dug into her blouse and glanced at the screen.

"Moron!" She popped up from the couch and stormed toward the windows to take the call.

Anxiety returned as De Theret reconsidered E.B.'s demand. He wasn't above removing people who were potential liabilities. But Samantha Newman was special. She had created his public image as an innovator, a lion of the new economy, everything he'd always wanted to be. Now, more than ever, he needed her.

She wasn't bad to look at either. Not that he would ever make a move for Samantha. Well, probably not. Anyway, keeping her at the company was just good business.

E.B. finished her conversation. An unpleasant one, by the looks of it.

"Who was that?" De Theret asked.

"Nobody to waste breath on." She dropped the phone into her cleavage and sauntered to the sofa. "Which brings me back to Samantha."

"Darling, please." He reached out his hand and pulled her down to sit beside him. "Remember when you were worried about Janna? You wanted me to fire her, too, and I told you that she would never come between us and our commitment to each other. And then, well, she died. It was sad, but . . . You see how life takes care of itself?"

"That wasn't 'life taking care of itself,' Vinnie."

"Sure it was." He stopped to contemplate what E.B might have meant.

Not wanting to pursue it, he changed the subject. "This thing with Lista Pearson makes me a little jumpy right now. With Janna gone, I let you take Lista under your wing, like you wanted. And now, she's—"

"A sad, stupid girl," E.B. said. "She knew what she was getting into."

"But I don't like these unforeseen events. Too many of them might call attention to the company, and not in a good way. And now, you want to get rid of Samantha, just when we may need her the most?" He started blinking again.

E.B. stroked his hand. "We have Derek now. He can work with me on our little projects and handle Samantha's job, too. He's so damned charming, he'll be a natural at PR. Eat it up like candy. We don't need her anymore, Vinnie. I want her gone."

"But—"

She stroked his thigh. "Never mind, now, Vinnie darling. I know you didn't mean to upset me. If you don't want to can her right now, I can work with that. I'll take care of everything. Like I always do for you, Vinnie. You like it when I take care of everything, don't you?"

The rhythmic strokes of her hand made De Theret lose his train of thought. E.B. was such a turn-on when she took control.

He pulled her to him. "I don't deserve you. I really don't. You're so good to me. And I'm so bad. I feel terrible that I upset you."

"Yes, you did, my bad little boy," she purred. "Bad boys like you need to be punished."

She had taken his cue, God bless her. He cowered in the corner of the couch, quaking with anticipation.

She stood and unbuttoned her blouse, letting it fall to the floor as she crossed to the bar.

She pressed a small button behind the blender. A panel slid open to reveal a small safe. Her fingers quickly worked the keypad. Three beeps, and the safe swung open.

He lowered himself to the carpet and crawled to the medallion in the center. He knew what would happen next.

She reached into the safe. "I have just the thing for you, my bad little Vinnie."

His eyes locked on the riding crop in her hand. He crouched lower. "I've been so bad, really, really bad. I have to be punished. Please."

She cracked the crop against her thigh and slowly sauntered toward him. Soon he would beg her to use it. But she would wait until he could stand it no longer, until he was at her mercy, helpless and needy.

Beyond the locked and soundproofed door, not even the night cleaning crew could hear the snap of the crop or De Theret's grateful moans through the thick, leather-padded walls.

CHAPTER FOURTEEN

Unmapped Territory

The maître d' led Samantha and Derek through the cheery hubbub of the popular wood-paneled dining room to their usual table near the window.

"Welcome back to Nino's."

Dolfo, their regular waiter, arrived almost immediately with a prosecco aperitivo, focaccia bread and olive tapenade.

Derek lifted his glass. "Here's to the body business. And to us."

Samantha stifled a groan and lowered her glass. "Please, let's not—"

"No, no. I didn't mean us, as in you and me, together. I meant . . . heck, we're both good guys!"

She allowed herself a tiny smile. "To the good guys, then."

"I'll drink to that." After a sip, he set the glass down. His face turned serious. "I want to say something, Sam, and then I promise I'll never broach the subject again."

She thought she knew what was coming, and she didn't want to hear it. Yet, it hadn't really been fair, the way she'd cut him out of her life with so little explanation. She probably owed it to him to hear him out, one last time. Reluctantly, she nodded.

"I'll always love you." He waved away her protest. "That's a given, whether you want me to or not. But I promise you two things, and they're good forever. One, I won't pressure you anymore to have things like they used to be. You can relax about that.

"Two, I now have and will continue to have a very busy social life in the way of female companionship. Life does go on here. I don't mean to throw it in your face or anything. I'm only telling you because you said we should see other people. Those were your terms. I just want you to know that I'm honoring them."

Tracing the upward path of bubbles with her fingertips, Samantha stared into her prosecco. Derek made it difficult, being so understanding. In truth, she would always love him, too. He'd been the one who helped her care about living again after her family died in the fire. She owed him so much, and he was too much of a gentleman to remind her of it, which endeared him to her even more.

But that was then, and this was now. The widening gap between his rising ambition and her growing doubts about De Theret International had stretched the bond between them to the breaking point.

Derek grinned in the candlelight. "Don't I get applause, or something? That was a hell of a speech I made, if I do say so myself."

She put on a smile. "Too much self-satisfaction leads to blindness, you know. Didn't they warn you about that when you hit puberty?"

"Guess I missed that class." He winked at her and motioned for the waiter.

Samantha only half-listened to a litany of off-the-menu specials. Her mind was busy searching for a way to get through dinner without another awkward moment.

She had hoped this would be the beginning of a new relationship between them. But building a friendship in the unmapped territory between love and indifference was proving to be difficult.

"So," Derek said after Dolfo left with their order, "what have you been up to these days?"

She took a gulp of prosecco. "Not much."

"What about those resumes I gave you? Any word?"

His question drew her back to the meeting with Carter Chapman. She tried to think of a plausible response. "Uh, no word yet. Thought I'd give them until Monday to make some choices."

"Not good. You should've called them today, put a little pressure on."

"I know how to do my job, Derek."

"Who are they, anyway?"

"They asked for anonymity."

He frowned. "All our clients are treated confidentially. Don't they know that?"

"I can't talk about it yet. Let's change the subject."

He shook his head. "Sometimes I think you've got more secrets than the CIA. If I can't know where my people's resumes went, who can?"

"Right now, nobody."

They were heading toward a familiar battleground.

He raised his hands in surrender. "Okay, okay. Tell me about it when you're ready. Just make sure my name's spelled right on the commission check."

"I will." She drained the rest of her glass and searched for something neutral to talk about.

Dolfo brought a small bowl of olives and a plate of shaved cheese to the table, and Derek ordered a bottle of Sangiovese to go with their food. They shared antipasto without talking until the wine was poured.

Derek tasted the sample in his glass and pronounced it perfect. "By the way, did you ever reach Lista?"

Samantha suppressed a groan. Another subject she'd hoped to avoid. She shook her head.

"I know you feel responsible for her, Sam. But Lista has a pretty checkered history—"

"Let's not start again about Lista." The couple at the next table looked her way. Samantha lowered her voice. "I know something bad is going on."

"But E.B. told you—"

"As if anything that woman says could be true."

An odd look crept across Derek's face. "But the police talked to her days ago. I'm sure they believed her."

"Lista would not have moved to Bogotá without telling me," Samantha insisted. "Even if she had, she'd be there by now. She'd be somewhere, instead of nowhere, at least."

"How about the FBI?"

Samantha almost choked on her wine.

Derek continued his train of thought. "If Lista did leave the country, the FBI should be able to track her down. Though you may not want to open that can of worms again."

She searched his face for a hint of suspicion but found none. "I'll think about it."

"Or maybe you should just let it go."

"You're right," she said. "Let's drop it."

"I'm right? Wow, I haven't heard that from you in a long time."

They fell into another uncomfortable silence. Wasn't there anything safe they could talk about?

She caught sight of Nino's owner approaching their table. He shook hands with Derek, but before they could exchange greetings, a crash of shattering plates cut through the restaurant. With an apologetic shrug, the owner left to investigate.

The brief interlude gave Samantha a chance to change the subject. "What's the good news we're celebrating tonight?"

Derek smiled. "Just my usual brilliance." Before he could elaborate, Dolfo arrived with another appetizer. The *carciofi alla giudia* looked inviting.

For the rest of the meal, they managed to hold a relatively normal conversation together. Derek did most of the talking, mostly about his latest business triumphs. He saved his good news for last.

"You are now looking at the new Vice President in charge of the South American project."

Samantha nearly choked on an olive. That had been E.B. Odom's ex-husband's job, before he disappeared.

She took a gulp of wine. "Great." She hoped she sounded sincere.

"I figure, when I get there, I'll see Lista and tell her how worried you are about her."

If Derek found Lista in South America, that would change everything. And maybe it would explain another mystery. "Has anyone told you what happened to Trey Odom?"

"No. Why?"

"Well, he was the last one to have the job. I thought maybe they'd explain to you why he just seemed to disappear from the company, like Lista."

Derek shrugged. "Don't know and don't care. People come and go. It's the nature of business. The important thing here is, I'm getting close to the real action. You should be happy for me."

She set her fork down. If tonight was any indication, she and Derek would never be able to be as close as they once were.

Tears welled in her eyes as she listened to him outline his new responsibilities, but he never noticed that she was the opposite of happy for him.

As she put the key in the lock on her front door, Samantha heard the land line ringing. Out of habit, Derek rushed in and answered.

"Samantha Newman's residence." His eyebrows knit. "Who's calling?"

He made a face and covered the receiver. "If this is a new suitor, he sounds kinda hostile." He handed the phone to Samantha.

Who would be calling so late? "Hello?"

"Ms. Newman, Carter Chapman here."

Fresh from the wine-drenched, exhausting evening, it took a moment for his name to register. When it finally did, she couldn't think of anything to say. Especially with Derek standing so close.

"Are you all right?" Chapman asked.

"Of course." Residual anger from their last conversation crept into her voice. "Why shouldn't I be? I just got home from dinner with a friend."

Chapman got to the point. "I'd like to see you as soon as possible. I have some things you need to look at."

She glanced at Derek. "Not tonight."

"What about tomorrow?"

"I don't have a car."

"I'll pick you up, around eleven-thirty."

"I don't think so." What could be so urgent that Carter Chapman would be calling at this hour? And what made him think she'd be willing to see him again?

With Derek standing there, conversation was difficult.

"I know you have somebody there," Chapman said. "I'll try to make this simple. If you need an excuse, let's call it a business lunch. We can drive to my ranch tomorrow. It's not far. Wear something comfortable."

"No."

"Ms. Newman, we really need to meet as soon as possible. I've come across information regarding the whereabouts of your friend."

"You found her?" Samantha shot a glance at Derek.

"We'll talk tomorrow," Chapman replied. "Eleven-thirty. It's a date."

"I . . . I'm not sure."

"Think about it. I'll be at your place to pick you up, either way."

She disconnected.

Derek grinned. "I see you haven't lost much time seeking company elsewhere, either. Hot date?"

"No. Just a . . . an acquaintance." She pretended to straighten a painting on the wall behind Derek.

"Who'd he find?"

"Find?"

"I heard you say, 'you found her.' You sounded pretty excited."

Samantha's mind raced to find a plausible answer. "Oh . . . his puppy! His puppy wandered off, and he was really worried. But he found her." The lie sounded pretty good. It gave her the courage to face him again.

"Thanks for dinner, Derek. And congratulations on your promotion. I hope it brings you everything you want."

To her relief, he accepted the dismissal without objection.

"Good night, doll. Thanks for coming out with me. See you Monday." He gave her a parting wink and kissed her on the cheek.

She shut the door and took a deep breath. It was a relief to be alone. After the tumultuous week, and the ups and downs of dinner with Derek, she was ready for some peace.

Despite leaving Chapman up in the air about tomorrow, she knew she would have to meet with him if she wanted to find Lista. He'd found something he wanted her to see. She climbed the stairs to her bedroom and wondered what it could possibly be.

Serenity Ranch

Samantha woke with mixed feelings about seeing Carter Chapman again. Yesterday, the man had tried to play her for a fool. But if she wanted to know what he'd discovered about Lista, she would have to play his game, at least for today.

Truth was, she needed to figure him out, too. Especially her reaction to him. Their appointment today wasn't a real date. But a picnic? If this was only about Lista, why was he dragging her to his ranch just to show her what he'd found? And why was she willing to play along?

She shrugged off her qualms. At least the outing would be an adventure. It sounded more interesting than fretting all weekend at home without a car.

She rummaged through her closet, looking for something to wear. Soft and feminine? Outdoorsy?

The growing pile of rejects on her bed reminded her of the long-forgotten social jitters she suffered every time she dressed for a high school dance.

Get a hold of yourself, girl. He'd said to dress comfortably.

She opened a drawer and pulled out her old khaki shorts and a thin white cotton sweatshirt. Comfortable enough.

By eleven, she was in her living room, ready, and in need of something to relieve her nervous energy for the next half-hour.

A jumble of snapshots from a recent vacation she and Derek had taken together lay on the coffee table. She had always made photo albums of their special times together, but it had been hard to face this last batch. After last night's dinner at Nino's, it somehow seemed right to complete the task.

She was deep into memories of the trip when the doorbell rang.

One look at Carter Chapman standing in her doorway and the ghost of Derek on a Yucatan beach evaporated. Handsome as Chapman the businessman had appeared in the lobby of the Lancaster hotel, Chapman the tanned and fit weekend guy was even more appealing.

And after all the fuss she'd made getting dressed, she had picked the exact twin to his attire. He stood before her in khaki shorts and a long-sleeved white cotton tee. She laughed.

"Did I forget to zip my fly?" Feigning mock horror, he reflexively covered himself, which made Samantha laugh harder. By the time she regained control, he had strolled into her living room.

He picked up a handful of snapshots from the floor. "You must have dropped these." He glanced at a photo before he handed it over. "Cancun?"

"Playa del Carmen."

"Nice." He pointed to a picture of Derek holding a pair of large coconuts to his chest. "Your brother, I suppose?"

"Sort of." Was this the beginning of another maddening interrogation? "You said you had information about Lista?"

"I do, at my ranch. I thought we'd enjoy a drive out to the country. We can talk about it there, and maybe have some lunch. It's a pretty day, and, I don't know about you, but I could use a little R-and-R."

Samantha tossed the photos onto the table. Whatever news Chapman had about Lista probably wasn't good. Maybe it could wait a little longer. "If I take you up on your offer, I hope I don't regret it."

He smiled. "You won't." Again, his warm brown eyes captured hers. "But before we go, please tell me why you laughed when you opened the door. I have to warn you, my feelings hurt easily."

"Oh, it's just that we're dressed like the Bobbsey twins. Look." She pointed at their matching ensembles. "It struck me funny."

"If you think that's funny, I have at least a few dozen terrible jokes to tell you on the way. Nobody, but nobody ever laughs at my jokes. I wasn't even trying, with the wardrobe thing."

For the first few miles of what turned out to be a long drive in his vintage, English racing green XKE convertible, Samantha learned why the IRS agent crossed the road, how many centipedes it takes to screw in a light bulb, and why a baseball team is like a stack of pancakes. Before long, she was pleading for mercy.

"Your lips say *non*, but your eyes, zay beg for more." His French accent was awful, yet somehow hilarious, especially since it came from the man who had seemed so cool in their first encounter.

She suppressed a smile. "You're wrong. My eyes say stop. Please."

He pulled the Jag to the shoulder and braked. "Let's see. Take off your sunglasses."

She removed them and summoned her iciest stare. He lowered his Ray Bans to take a look. The moment his eyes struck hers, her face heated. She pushed her shades back on.

He slid his up again and steered the car onto the road again. "Your eyes are green, just like I remembered. Green means go."

"That only counts with traffic signals." She surveyed the unfamiliar scenery. "Speaking of going, where are we?"

"About halfway there."

"Where's there?"

"My place isn't too far from Brenham. I couldn't think of a better place to go for a picnic today. Hope you don't mind."

She leaned back against the leather seat. In her search for Lista, she had found a new mystery: Carter Chapman. He had seemed genuinely human when he apologized for botching their lunch meeting. But was he completely for real?

Wavering between doubt and curiosity, she decided to let the day play out.

"Drive on." She shut her eyes and let the wind whip through her hair.

"Ms. Newman? Samantha? We're here."

Chapman's voice came through a tiny slit in the darkness. Her eyes fluttered open. She sat up, blinking at the sunlight.

"Oh, gosh," she sputtered. "I fell asleep. How embarrassing! I'm so sorry."

"I'm the one who should apologize. I didn't realize how boring my jokes really were."

"You're sweet to try to make me feel better, but I'm really sorry. I haven't slept well lately, and I . . . well, I guess I relaxed for a few minutes."

"That's good." He got out of the car and opened her door. "Welcome to my home."

Her eyes followed the sweep of his arm. Low hills, thickly carpeted in alternating swaths of bluebonnets and Indian paintbrush, rolled out in every direction. Bees hovered over the nodding flowers, their busy wings sparkling in the sun. The sky was startlingly blue, with a few puffy white clouds punctuating the expanse. The honeyed scent of spring hung in the soft air.

Samantha had never seen countryside as lovely as this. The beauty of it stung her eyes. "Oh my."

"Glad you like it. After lunch we can go exploring, if you want to."

Her gaze swept across the hills again. It was almost too perfect to take in.

Chapman smiled down at her. "Tell you what. Dottie can bring our food to the porch, if you want to stay out here to eat."

She tore her eyes away from the scenery and looked at him. Dottie?

Her mind snapped back to the reason she was here. This place was lovely, and Chapman was good-looking, but he was only doing a job, albeit in a very unorthodox way. She reminded herself that this wasn't a real date. It was silly to let herself imagine.

She shook off the reverie. Might as well get the whole thing over. She turned toward the house to follow him.

The white three-story mansion, a classic Texas Greek revival, stood like a temple at the crest of the hill, with native stone steps leading up to a wide veranda. Giant magnolias flanked the corners of the house. The carved oak doorway was framed by Greek columns that continued around the building every ten feet or so along the veranda. By any measure, it was a grand edifice.

Chapman led her up the steps and through the front door. "It's kind of pretentious, for a little old Texas ranch house, I know. I bought the property when I sold my first software company. The house came with it, so I had to learn to live with it." He grinned.

A two-story rotunda formed the ceiling of the grand entry hall, with a grand staircase spiraling up to a second and third floor.

Samantha craned her neck to take it in. "Incredibly gorgeous. I'm impressed."

His eyes locked onto hers. "That makes two of us."

She caught herself daydreaming again. *Snap out of it. Remember why you're here.*

A middle-aged woman appeared at a doorway on the other side of the entry. Except for the lop-sided bun atop her head, her gray/blue eyes and sturdy build, she resembled a countrified version of Gertie.

She wiped her hands on her apron. "Either I'm early, or you're late." She turned and disappeared through the door with a good-natured chuckle.

Chapman took Samantha by the hand and followed the woman into the next room, which turned out to be a large farmhouse kitchen.

A high ceiling and miles of counters and cabinets wrapped two sides of the room. Shiny pots of all shapes and sizes hung above a cooking island that extended to a food preparation counter where two pubescent children, a boy and a girl, sat on stools.

The boy was snapping fresh green beans in half and dropping them into a bowl. The girl, who seemed a bit older, cut long, narrow strips of dough for the top of what looked like a fresh apple pie. They did not look up when Samantha and Chapman entered.

The woman who had greeted them stood at the sink scrubbing potatoes.

Chapman grabbed a raw bean from the bowl and chewed on it. "Lunch doesn't look ready to me."

"This is supper," the woman said without turning from the sink. "Lunch was ready at lunchtime. It's darn near two o'clock."

"Sorry." He raised his voice above the slosh of running water. "Dottie, I want you to meet someone. Samantha, this is Dottie Velasco. Dottie, Samantha Newman."

Dottie shut the water off. Wiping her hands on her apron, she turned to greet Samantha.

"Oh, you're a pretty one!" A warm smile crinkled the corners of her eyes. "Sorry about before. I've been goin' through the change o' life lately, and the crabbiness comes over me at the most peculiar times."

Samantha took the woman's damp, pink hand into hers. "Pleased to meet you, Dottie." She seemed too old to be Chapman's wife. "Sorry we're late."

"Oh, not to worry. Lunch is in that hamper over there. You did say a picnic?"

"I did." Chapman grabbed the basket. "Only I think we'll rough it on the porch this afternoon. We'll be out there in case you want to bring us any more delicacies from the kitchen, like this apple pie, when it's ready."

"There's pecan pie in the hamper, if it ain't ruined from being packed up too long." Dottie shook her head. "Sorry. There I go again. You two get on outta here and enjoy lunch, before I turn into the Wicked Witch. Go on now."

Chapman started toward the door and motioned for Samantha to follow, but she held back to watch the children work at their kitchen chores.

"Oh, I'm sorry, kids," he said. "I almost forgot to introduce you. Samantha, this is Courtney and Kerry."

"Hi," the two adolescents said in shy unison.

"Hello." She studied their faces. So, Dottie was not Chapman's wife. But who were these children?

Chapman guided her through a side door onto the shady veranda. Outside the white baluster railing, a moss-banked creek coursed along a gentle curve. On the opposite bank, willow trees leaned their delicate branches over the water. She followed the lazy flow of the water until it bent around a corner and disappeared.

Chapman arranged their food on a wrought iron table. "Looks like Dottie kept the menu simple. Hope you don't mind."

Samantha considered the cold roast turkey, corn and bean salad, spiced peaches, jalapeno bread, and what looked like homemade pecan pie.

"Look's better than anything I'd be eating at home today."

He extracted a chilled bottle of white wine from the hamper, poured two glasses and handed one to her.

She gestured toward the water. "That stream comes so close to the house. Does it ever flood around here?"

"Actually, I put it here on purpose. I wanted to have a swimming pool, but I didn't want it to ruin the old-fashioned ambience of the estate. Luckily, I found a guy who designed the perfect solution: a pool that looks like a natural creek. It wraps around this side and the back of the house. The back is in the sun, and this side, well . . ." His hand swept across the willow canopy overhanging the water. "It has a solar-powered current, so it always looks like it's flowing. I don't usually go in for artificial things, but this seemed like a reasonable compromise."

"It's really lovely." She raised her glass. "Here's to your place in the country."

"To Serenity," he said. "That's the name of it. Serenity Ranch."

"To Serenity," she echoed. Their eyes locked again.

He broke contact first and backed away. "Let's eat, for goodness sake, or Dottie will never cook for us again. Sit, and enjoy."

During lunch, Chapman talked mostly about the history of the surrounding area. Samantha listened patiently, but as soon as they had drained the last drops of wine from the bottle, Samantha broached a subject that had been bugging her since they sat down.

"The children I met in the kitchen, are they . . .?"

"Dottie's? Oh, no. They're her grandchildren."

"But, are they . . ."

He finally caught up. "Mine?" His expression darkened. "No. Not mine. They're Ralph's, Dottie's son. He's the ranch caretaker, among other things."

"Your chauffeur, I suppose?" That would explain the seemingly preposterous story he had told her on the day they met.

"And my sometime chauffeur, yes."

An awkward silence fell before he continued. "Ralph needed a fresh start a few years back, after he testified against one of his former employers back East. I was doing work for the government then, too, and when they asked if I would help, I offered him a job here. They murdered his wife before he could move her, but he made it here with his mother and his children. They're good people, and I think they're comfortable here. He does good work. Not to mention Dottie's cooking. They're like family now." A wave of sadness swept across his face.

"Sorry," she said, "I didn't mean to pry."

"It's okay." He tossed his napkin onto the table and stood up. "Let's take a walk."

She followed him around the veranda toward the back of the house. He led her across a small footbridge that spanned the swimming creek, then down a slight slope and up again toward a gentle rise.

At the top, they started down again, crossing through a field of bluebonnets with bees buzzing harmlessly at their ankles. It seemed like a well-worn path.

He moved a few paces ahead, toward a manicured patch of green that was bordered by a low fence and marked by four giant live oaks, one at each corner.

He waited for her to catch up. "I want to show you something."

It was a small, neatly kept graveyard. An old stone monument that bore the name Eldridge stood opposite a much newer one with three names engraved on it.

Her breath caught as she took in the words.

Katherine Chapman, 1979–2012, beloved wife of Carter Chapman and mother of Margaret and Michael, 2001–2012. Together in birth. Together in death.

Tears brimmed in her eyes.

"You asked about my family." His voice wavered as he spoke. "This is where they are. They were killed by a drunk driver just outside of Houston. Killed instantly, all of them." His jaw clenched.

"The original owner of the place erected the other monument. The family plot and the oaks were staked and planted then, too, though none of the family was ever buried here. It seemed like the perfect spot to bring my family back to. It was ours, after all."

She stood beside him and contemplated the graves. He had survived a terrible personal tragedy. She knew what that was like.

After a long silence, he spoke. "Let's get Dottie to make us some coffee. We still have business to take care of."

"Lista." She looked up at him. "Did you find her?"

"Not yet, but I'm getting closer. Let's get back, and I'll show you what I have."

CHAPTER SIXTEEN

Dear Sam

Samantha surveyed the library from the comfort of a soft leather sofa near the fireplace. Late afternoon light filtered through the windows, bathing the wood-paneled room in a saffron cloud. Floor-to-ceiling bookshelves spanned the walls.

She ran her toe along the Persian rug and contemplated the meaning of the three graves. The sadness in Chapman's eyes at their first encounter now had an explanation. Despite the beauty surrounding him, there was an emptiness impossible to fill.

Near the bay window that overlooked the front veranda, Chapman removed a large document holder from the drawer of an antique desk and brought it with him to the sofa.

"I'm afraid I don't have good news about your friend."

She searched his face for a clue. "Is she . . .?" She couldn't bear to finish the question.

"Her exact situation is still unknown. But we found some items possibly belonging to her."

Samantha could hardly breathe. "Where?"

"New Orleans."

"New Orleans?" She lapsed into silence while a thought was forming. "De Theret has offices in New Orleans."

"I know. I've been following De Theret for some time. I probably know more than you do about the company by now. But I haven't been able to prove anything. That's why I'm interested in your friend's disappearance. It may help me with a situation of my own."

She stood and began pacing the length of the carpet and back. "But if Lista was working for De Theret in New Orleans, why didn't she tell me? Why did E.B. insist that she'd sent her to Bogotá? And why didn't they announce her transfer, like they usually do when someone gets moved to another office?"

"I think I know the answer, though it's just a theory right now," he said. "It involves the investigation I started long before you contacted the FBI."

He hesitated. "Why don't you sit down? This is kind of a long story."

"No thanks. I'm fine."

"Some of this could be pretty tough on you."

"Don't let that stop you. I'm pretty tough myself."

He set the folder on a side table and continued.

"As you know, De Theret International has been a huge financial success. But the bulk of that success doesn't come from its staffing services anymore. There are two far more lucrative operations that fuel the De Theret engines."

She stopped pacing and faced him. "You're going to tell me it's something illegal, aren't you?"

"You don't seem surprised."

"Oddly enough, I'm not. I've suspected it for a while now. After I worked so hard to build a career at De Theret, I guess I wasn't willing to let any negative thoughts interfere. But when Lista disappeared, I couldn't stand by and do nothing."

Tears filled her eyes. "I'm afraid I stayed quiet too long."

"I'd say your reaction was pretty normal."

"Common maybe, but I wouldn't call it normal. If I'd spoken up earlier, maybe Lista wouldn't be—"

"Let's not go down that road. We're not sure of anything, yet."

Samantha shook her head. "Lista was always kind of a lost person, solitary and insecure. She was a good friend to me when my family died, so when she needed me, I tried to help her through. She'd come running to my office almost every day in tears over something E.B. had said or done to her. That woman can play such cruel mind games.

"Anyway, after Lista disappeared, I knew I had to find her." She wiped the tears streaking down her face. "Go on. You have more to tell me, I'm guessing."

"Well, there is, and there isn't. We know that De Theret has offices in cities that correlate with some high-priced call girl operations."

"You think Lista was involved with—"

"We don't know for sure. But items of hers were found in a hotel room that was registered to a man who used an alias. He's also disappeared. And given her past . . ."

Samantha's heart skipped a beat. "Her past?"

"We know she worked her way through college as a female escort."

How could they know that? Lista was never arrested. There was no record. Unless . . .

Chapman read her thoughts. "There was a court case, against a guy named Angelo Infante, for racketeering. Lista Pearson's name appeared in the file."

A giant sinkhole opened beneath her. Samantha's name was in that file, too. How on earth had Chapman found it? What did it tell him about her? Did he think she was involved . . . like Lista?

He'd reeled her in with his sad eyes and silly jokes, making her think he liked her, all the while setting her up to trust him, all the while believing she was . . .

Embarrassment and shame washed over her. She couldn't bring herself to look at him. She had to get out of there. "I've heard enough. If you can't tell me where Lista is right now, then I need to go home."

"I want you to see something first. Please."

He withdrew a clear plastic evidence sleeve from the document holder. "The original copy of this was inside a purse that was found in the hotel room. There was no wallet or phone, so it would help if you could identify the handwriting."

Inside the sleeve was what looked like a letter. What did it have to do with Lista? She moved to snatch it out of his hand, but he pulled it away. "I'd like to give you some background before you see it."

She crossed her arms to steel herself. "Go ahead."

"There was an incident at a hotel in New Orleans. It's not completely clear what happened, but there are a few clues. Among them are a piece of luggage and the purse with this letter addressed to 'Sam' inside.

"Police were looking for a man named Sam, but when I saw the signature, I thought it might relate to the message you sent the FBI about your missing friend." He handed it to her.

Dear Sam, it began.

"It's to me! Lista wrote a letter to me!" She started pacing again.

"You recognize the handwriting?"

"Yes, it's Lista's." She continued reading.

You've probably been worried, because you know how I can get myself in trouble sometimes. Well, here I go again, only now, you're not here to help. It's OK, though, because this time I'm going to pull myself out and start over where I belong.

I'm going home, where that she-devil E.B. can't bother me. I refuse to be her puppet anymore. I'm going to finish my teaching degree, find a man to marry, and love him until the day I die.

When I get back to Nebraska, I'll call and let you know my address. Wish me luck! I'm going to do it right this time.

Samantha struggled to read the rest. By the time she reached the last sentence, tears were streaming down her cheeks again. She squeezed her eyes shut, but the flow would not be stemmed.

Chapman handed her a box of tissues.

She gave the letter back to him and wiped her face.

He returned the letter to the folder. "Interesting that she wrote to you, instead of calling, or texting."

"She's probably still using a company phone. Nothing's private when you work for De Theret. But maybe she's home now, like she said, in Nebraska."

"I don't think so," he replied. "She had a flight booked, but there was no ticket in the purse, and she never boarded the plane. Her family hasn't heard from her in months."

Samantha's breath left her. "It doesn't look good, does it?"

"No."

"Anything else?" She braced herself for what might come next.

"Why don't you sit down? You look a little pale."

"No thanks."

Chapman glanced at the document holder. "I have something else to show you. But it can wait."

She put on a brave face. "I might as well see everything."

He passed a folder to her. A set of two documents were inside. "These are copies of papers that were found in the luggage. They appear to be personnel files from De Theret International. I'd like you to take look."

A quick glance through them was enough. "They're the personnel files of Trey Odom and Janna Donald." Slowly, something dawned on her. "They're the two others. The ones who disappeared before Lista. But why—?"

He echoed her question. "Why would she have these particular files in her bag? Maybe they contain something important. Another piece of the puzzle. What do you know about them?"

Whatever Chapman knew—or thought he knew—about the past she and Lista shared wasn't as important as finding out what happened to her.

Samantha needed to concentrate. Lista took those files for a reason. What was it?

She lowered herself into a side chair beside the sofa and shared her thoughts out loud.

"Janna Donald was the first V.P. of Personnel for De Theret. She was his girlfriend. They'd lived together for years before he started the company. That's what was weird about her disappearance. Nobody had more job security than Janna. But one day, out of the blue, Vinson sent a memo saying Janna had retired. She was only about thirty-eight or nine."

"Did he explain?"

"He said she had moved back to Chicago, where she was from. That's when he promoted E.B. to Janna's job. It didn't take long to figure it out that E.B. had replaced Janna in other ways too, if you know what I mean."

"E.B.? Are you referring to Eula Beth Bewley Odom?"

"Yes. How did you know?"

"Odom is the one we think is running the call girl operation. Apparently, she uses high-priced hookers to lure valuable corporate accounts into signing contracts with De Theret for all their staffing business. She advertises the escort services under different names in each city. And my hunch is that she hides the profits in the books of the Elite Professionals division. It's probably where she recruits the girls from, too. Very slick."

"That's one way to describe her."

"You said Trey Odom also disappeared? E.B.'s husband?"

"Yes. But after she hooked up with De Theret, she left poor Trey. He stuck around, though, when De Theret tapped him to run the South American division. I guess the money was too good to pass up. Trey was gone a lot, but he always showed up for quarterly meetings, until the last two. Now they don't even mention his name."

"I am familiar with their South American operation," Chapman said. "It's almost certainly a front for low-level drug smuggling, which is the other business I've been investiga—"

Samantha felt the blood drain from her face. "Derek!"

"Derek Grey?" Chapman had done his homework.

"Derek is the new head of the South American operation. He told me last night at dinner. It hasn't had a president since Trey, and now . . . Derek is so excited about it."

Her mind raced. Please, not Derek! She didn't trust him like she once had, but only because of his allegiance to De Theret. She would never let herself believe that he'd be involved in something criminal. He wouldn't have shared the excitement over his promotion so openly with her.

Maybe he didn't know what was going on. Maybe they were just using him. He should be warned. The urge to flee returned.

She popped off the sofa, juiced with adrenaline. "Derek Grey is not a criminal! He's always been ambitious, maybe a little too much. But he wouldn't do anything like . . ."

She shook her head to banish the idea. "And Lista? Whatever she did in college, she'd put it behind her. We were all trying to find our way back then. I'd believe anything of E.B., and even Vinson De Theret, but Derek and Lista?"

She was beside herself. "You want me to accept that Derek and Lista, my friends, are pushing drugs and prostitution? You're crazy! You're all wrapped up in some cops and robbers fantasy. These are my friends!"

Chapman tried to calm her. "It's just a theory at the moment, but it's only a matter of time—"

"Stop it!" She covered her ears and paced the length of the room and back, each step propelling her to a higher level of anger. She turned and confronted him.

"I know they're not perfect angels, but what you're saying can't be true. You think you know everything about them and everything about me. But you're wrong."

She dropped into the chair and buried her face in her hands.

Chapman stood. "Why don't we take a break?"

She wiped tears from her face. "I can't do this anymore. I need to go home."

When she made a move to leave, he stopped her. "Please, there's only a bit more. If you need a breather, take a few minutes. I can show you another trail outside. Go alone, if you like."

She wanted the pain to stop. But if she insisted on going home now, she'd be stuck in a car with Chapman for the long drive, and she wasn't ready to be that close to him again. Maybe it was better to stay, hear him out and rip the scab off in one go. But she needed a breather first.

She followed him to the front porch. He pointed toward a path that disappeared into a stand of oaks. "Take all the time you want."

Barely able to put one foot in front of the other, she slumped down the steps and picked up the trail.

She'd been stupid to believe that Carter Chapman liked her, respected her, trusted her. Beyond what she could do to help him solve the case he'd been working on before they met, it was ridiculous to think he was interested in her. He probably didn't give a hoot.

She'd spent years running from past sorrows, building an independent life she could be proud of. Her family's tragedy and how she'd coped with it were buried deep. But Chapman had unearthed all of it and would probably use it to his advantage. How much did he know? And what could he really understand?

Late afternoon light was fading by the time she made her way back up the trail to the house. There was no sign of Chapman in the library.

She flopped onto the sofa, numb. She wanted to go home, but she didn't have the energy to move. Chapman would come looking for her soon enough.

There was more to tell her, he'd said. Maybe it wasn't too late. Maybe Lista was okay. She rested her head on a throw pillow and drifted into oblivion.

CHAPTER SEVENTEEN

Use Me

From his desk in the library, Carter Chapman watched Samantha's slow, labored breathing.

Every inch of him itched to get De Theret, to bring his company down, watch him crumble under the weight of his own filthy life. Before he met Samantha, he was sure she was part of it. He had hoped to pressure her into making a deal and turn her into a key witness.

It had been a straightforward plan, until she became more than a name in a file. She was flesh and blood, and her remorse over delaying the urge to blow the whistle seemed genuine. Seeing her curled up like a child on his sofa, it was hard to imagine how she could be involved.

The room had grown dark. He pulled a cashmere throw off a chair to cover her and went to tell Dottie not to worry about dinner.

Her son, Ralph, was alone at the kitchen counter, eating pie. Chowing down on his mother's irresistible food never seemed to alter his naturally wiry frame.

"Where's your Mom?" Chapman asked.

"Quilting club. She asked me to stick around and help with dinner. It's already cooked. I just have to take it out of the oven. Hope you don't mind, I helped myself to a little pie from lunch."

Chapman grinned. "Don't worry. I won't tell your mommy on you."

"Thanks, man. Ready for dinner?"

"I don't think we'll be having dinner tonight. She fell asleep in the library. My guess is she won't feel like eating, even if she wakes up before morning."

"Is it her friend, the one you're looking for in New Orleans?"

Chapman nodded.

"I guess that helps make your case."

"It fills in some blanks, but . . . I may have to take a different tack."

"How's that?"

"I'm not sure I can use her like I'd planned."

"She won't cooperate?"

"No, that's not it. She's just different from the picture I got when I studied her file."

"You mean the stuff in that old trial record?"

"Yes. Something about her doesn't jive. It's hard to reconcile that information with the person in front of me."

"Sometimes people aren't the same as what they seem to be on paper," Ralph said. "I worked for bad guys once. But I wasn't one of them. Maybe it's like that. Or, maybe she's changed."

Chapman shook his head. "Right now, I'm not sure what to think."

"So, is it time for Plan B?"

"Not until I have a Plan B."

Ralph chuckled. "You always have a Plan B. Want me to dish out some pot roast while you fill me in?"

"No thanks. I'll just go upstairs and try to rethink this thing."

"I changed the security code like you wanted."

"Good."

"And I put the new software on your laptop. Should be done installing by now. The rest of the system is up and running, too. If you don't need me, I'll put the food away and head home."

"Thanks." Chapman eyed the solitary wedge of pecan pie left in the tin. "On second thought, that pie looks really good."

He made himself a large mug of coffee, grabbed a fork and the rest of the pie, and headed upstairs.

Samantha awoke to a symphony of chirping birds. The smell of baking bread was everywhere.

She unfurled her stiff body and sat up. Her eyes were hot and sticky. The unfamiliar room confused her, until she remembered where she was, and why. Dread grabbed her throat.

Her fears had come true. Something *was* rotten at the core of the company. And Lista was in trouble, if she was even still alive. And Derek could be in danger, too.

A lamp was still lit over the library desk. She wrapped the cashmere throw around her aching shoulders, got up and turned it off. The room glowed pink with early sunlight.

"You're awake." Carter Chapman's voice came from somewhere near the door.

"Not sure I'm fully conscious." Her tongue was thick and uncooperative. "But I'm not dreaming anymore, am I?"

"Why don't we leave that conversation until after breakfast? Dottie's got some killer cinnamon rolls in the oven, and the coffee's made."

"Mmmm, coffee," she mumbled. "Is there somewhere I can freshen up?"

"There's a guest room upstairs. When you reach the second floor, turn left. First door on the right. There's a toothbrush, toothpaste, everything you need."

"A regular B&B."

"We aim to please. Take your time."

Sunlight streamed through the window over the kitchen sink. Samantha studied Chapman as he refilled her coffee and topped off his own. Though he was being exceptionally polite, she had a pretty good idea of what he really thought of her. Still, she faced another hour or two with him. Best to keep her guard up until she could get home.

Coffee would help. She took a sip. "So, what's next?"

Chapman plated a cinnamon roll and handed it to her. "I'm not sure."

"You must have some kind of plan."

"What I had in mind won't work now."

"Why not?"

"I have to rethink a few things."

"Why?"

He stared into his coffee mug.

She tried gain. "Does it have something to do with me?"

When he still didn't answer, she forged ahead. "Look, I don't know what your plan was, but here's what I think. The easiest way to find Lista and uncover what's really happening at De Theret is to use me. I'm still on the inside, for now anyway. Let me find out what I can."

"No!" His harsh tone startled her. "You cannot be involved. You should never step foot in that building again."

"Who are you, my father?" She set her mug down harder than she'd meant to. Coffee splashed onto the table.

Chapman looked stunned.

Her sudden anger took her by surprise, too. But rage felt good. Better than despair.

So what if she'd made a fool of herself yesterday? So what if he had excavated her past and thought he understood her history?

"I will not crawl into a shell and let other people get hurt. I have to find Lista, with or without your help. Besides, what would look more suspicious— going to work as usual, or never showing up again? Or is it that you don't trust me."

He blanched. "I don't want you to put yourself in danger, Ms. Newman. These are nasty people."

She popped out of her chair. "I've worked with these people for years, Mr. Chapman. I know how to handle them. and I owe it to Lista to . . . to . . ."

Her energy gave out. She sat again and pressed on.

"I know you planned to use me in some way when you set up that ridiculous meeting at the Lancaster. Otherwise, you wouldn't have put on that stupid charade about being Roland what's-his-name. I'm saying it's okay. Use me. I feel like a victim, too, and I don't like it. I have to help. I can carry it off. I was an actress in my college days. Did you know that?"

"It may have come up in the research."

She winced. That blasted file. Once this was over, she would set the record straight.

"You had it right from the beginning," she said. "I will make a good spy."

"I don't want—"

"I'm tired of talking about it." She rose from the table. "Serenity is beautiful, but I don't feel like trying to enjoy myself right now. I want to go home."

She took his silence for acquiescence. "Please thank Dottie for me. I'll be waiting in the car." She left him alone with nothing to argue.

The drive back to Houston was excruciating, made worse by the extended silence between them. When Chapman's Jag came to a stop in front of Samantha's house, the two of them lingered for an awkward moment, neither one knowing how to say goodbye.

His hand reached for hers and squeezed it gently.

She pulled away and opened the car door to get out. "Don't worry. I'll be fine."

"Ms. Newman . . . Samantha . . . I can't tell you how sorry I am about—"

Before he could finish, she shut the door and walked away.

CHAPTER EIGHTEEN

Boom

After the emotional upheaval of the weekend, by the time Monday morning dawned, Samantha felt like a stretched-out rubber band that was close to snapping. She struggled through a brain fog to get ready in time for Gertie to pick her up.

As they drove to the office, Gertie gave her a side-glance. "You okay?"

"I'm fine."

"If you say so. Oh, before I forget, the ten o'clock management meeting was moved up to nine."

Samantha groaned. "At least I can get it over with early."

Walking into her office felt like she was entering a wholly different space, even though the desk, credenza, and chairs were the same as the ones she left on Friday, the carpet was still mauve, and the view outside the window, identical. But there was a strangeness, somehow, as if it had been cloned and then teleported to an alien galaxy.

Or maybe I'm the alien.

After last week's barrage of highs and lows, she was in a kind of altered consciousness.

To say that she was weary was an understatement. To kill the ten minutes before her meeting started, she went through the motions of a usual Monday morning: boot up the computer, scroll through new messages, delete, delete, mark for later. She couldn't focus on any of it.

It was almost nine. She took a deep breath, picked up the meeting agenda and headed for the executive conference room.

The otherworldly feeling stayed with Samantha as she took her usual place at the black marble conference table. The distance between her and the others in the room felt like light-years.

Once upon a time, they had all shared a common goal: to make De Theret International a success. Now there was nothing to share, except the years of work she wished she'd never been part of.

"Samantha?" Vinson De Theret broke her isolation.

He'd been talking to her, had asked her a question. Her brain tried to recall what her ears had heard. Nothing registered.

She scanned the faces of those seated around the table for a clue. De Theret, Derek, Kevin Molton, all stared back at her. All except E.B., who seemed engrossed in the close scrutiny of the diamond on her shiny red fingernail.

It was no use. "Sorry. Guess I wasn't listening."

E.B. giggled.

The back of Samantha's neck prickled.

Derek leaned over and whispered. "The special client you're working on. From the files I gave you. I told V.D. about them, and he wants to know what's happening with them."

Her mind raced in search of an answer.

"Uh . . . nothing yet."

"Nothing?" De Theret's eyebrows shot up. His pale irises were nearly iridescent under the fluorescent lighting.

She felt her face heat. Her boss was accustomed to getting rapid results, especially from her. At the very least, he expected a more elaborate answer.

She felt the sting of his displeasure. "I'll call them to see where we stand."

"Let me know." De Theret's tone dripped with reproach.

Now that she was hyper-alert, she hoped to hear a discussion of the South American operation. But there was none. Feeling less than brave after her gaffe, she decided not to ask about it. Perhaps it had been mentioned while she was in her self-absorbed fog.

When the meeting was over, Derek followed her out. "Are you okay?"

His solicitous tone rankled her. "Why shouldn't I be?"

"You seem a little on edge. More than usual. Anyway, wanna grab some lunch?"

"No thanks. I'm going to get my car out of the shop. I'll just grab something on the way back."

"Why don't we get a quick bite? I'll take you to get your car afterward."

"I called the van to pick me up."

"Call and tell them you have a ride."

"Derek!" E.B. Odom's voice sliced into their conversation. She caught up with them near the elevator.

"You and I are discussing that new project during lunch today." Her eyes shot daggers at him.

Derek seemed torn. "Well, I suppose I can just drop Sam off at the car place, then come back and do lunch with you."

Both women protested, but Derek cut them off.

"I insist. You may not know this, E.B., but it's kind of a ritual, taking Sam to get her car out of the shop. My week would be incomplete without it. I'll be back in a sec."

He turned to Samantha. "Let's just leave from here." He pushed the elevator button to the parking garage.

Before either woman could argue, the elevator opened, and Derek led Samantha in. As the doors were closing, he waved goodbye to E.B. She did not look happy.

"Fourteen hundred dollars! For what?"

Samantha scanned the hieroglyphs on the repair ticket. "I don't understand. What happened to the twelve hundred I paid you last month to fix it?"

The cashier yawned. "It's all down there, Miss."

Derek was driving away, but Samantha caught his eye and waved him back. He pulled his car into an empty space and joined her at the booth.

"What's up?"

"This bill. I can't believe the car needed all this stuff after the work they've done already."

Derek looked over the invoice. "Well, it's easy enough to see if they replaced these parts. Where's the car?"

The cashier gestured to the other side of the garage and handed Derek the key.

He walked over to the car, got in and pulled it up next to the booth. Leaving the engine to idle, he got out and popped the hood.

The shop owner appeared inside the booth, wiping his grease-stained hands on a rag. "You got a question about the bill, Ms. Newman?"

"Yes, Barney. I don't see how the car needed so much work when it's been in your shop practically every week this month."

Barney turned to the cashier. "Let's see the ticket."

The young woman shrugged. "She got it already."

"Oh. . . I gave it to my friend." Just as Samantha turned to get the receipt from Derek, something flashed under the car.

A loud pop followed. Derek raised up. His eyes locked on Samantha's just before a deafening blast hurled her backward with the force of a cannon.

She slammed hard against the cashier's booth. Then everything went black.

CHAPTER NINETEEN

Pain

She is in the car repair shop. Something is wrong. E.B. is attacking her.

E.B. pushes, pulls, tears at her skin with those scarlet claws. Her face! Her eyes!

E.B. vanishes.

She runs to the mirror. It isn't her own face. It's Lista's face! She grabs at the skin, tries to pull off Lista's face. It doesn't feel like skin. Horrible . . . dry and stiff, like . . .

Now she is back in her college dorm room. Someone says her parents are dead.

She hears screaming . . . screaming . . .

"Hey! She's coming out of it! Hold her arms. Quick! Push the IV."

Someone is talking. She tries to open her eyes, but everything is blackness.

"There now. Feeling better?"

She struggles to answer. Her voice sounds strange.

Soon, she is inside another dream.

A warm hand wrapped around Samantha's.

"Aawah?" Her tongue felt like a wad of dry cotton.

"It's okay. I'm here."

The voice sounded familiar. Carter Chapman? What was he doing there? Where was she?

"Whaaa . . .?"

She tried to force her eyes open. Everything remained black, and the effort sent pain shooting through her head. She reached up to try to figure out what was wrong. Her fingers touched a thick pad taped over the top half of her face. "Whaa . . .?"

"You'll be all right," Chapman said gently. "You had a few slivers of glass in your eyes, but they're out now. The doctors say there should be no permanent damage. They want to keep you bandaged and quiet for a few more days."

It took a while for her to absorb the information. "Whaaa?" she tried to ask again. It was hard to think, to speak. "Whaaa happ . . .?"

"Well, your head will probably hurt for a bit. You have a pretty bad concussion. You were out for quite a while. Other than that, some soreness and a few cuts and bruises, they say you're okay."

Her head felt like hot, thick pudding. She tried again. "Whaaa happen?"

"You don't remember?"

She tried to think, but nothing made it through the haze. "No."

"Your car. It exploded."

She tried to relate his words to something in her memory. Her car. Exploded? Where was she when it happened? What made it happen? Why? She tried to think, but the answers would not come.

She shook her head in frustration. Fresh pain bridged the space between her ears and lifted her off the pillows. "Oww!"

Chapman took her by the shoulders and gently lowered her down. "Take it easy. You need to stay quiet so you can heal. It'll clear up in time."

There were muffled sounds of someone else in the room, the rustle of cloth, the soft clack of plastic on plastic, the crinkle of paper.

"The nurse is here," Chapman told her. "She's going to give you something for the pain. Just take it easy. I'll be here when you wake up."

There was nothing to do but acquiesce. The nurse said something. Then a slow, gentle release washed over her.

Days were a timeless fog. Samantha became minimally aware of the comings and goings of the hospital staff, the smell of antiseptic, and Chapman's constant presence.

At last, she was stronger. It was time to remove her bandages. In the dimness of her darkened hospital room, she could make out his face smiling down at her.

"Good afternoon," he said. "Nice to see you looking so good."

"Nice to see you, period."

He put his hand on hers. His touch was very familiar. Faint memory pushed through to her consciousness. He'd been with her, holding her hand—for days, as if he'd been worried about her. As if he cared.

"Feel okay?"

"Pretty sore. I'd like to get out of here and see some sunshine."

He poured water into a plastic cup, added a straw and offered it to her.

"No thanks," she said. "I'm ready to handle something a little more interesting."

"Martini?"

"I was thinking more along the lines of a steak," she said. "But I'd settle for a smoothie."

She adjusted the bed to sit up, but it made her head spin. She lowered it halfway down again. Chapman helped her rearrange the pillows.

She was glad to have the bandages off, but there was still a big blank where her memory should be. When she tried to retrieve pieces of what had happened to her from the recesses of her brain, nothing budged.

The last thing she remembered was that awful Monday morning meeting. Anything after that had been wiped away.

She frowned. "Where was I when my car exploded?"

"At the repair shop."

"At the shop? I wasn't driving somewhere?"

"No. It exploded at the shop."

Strange, asking about something that she'd experienced but couldn't recall. The repair shop. She tried to add this piece of information to her memory to see if it connected with anything. No luck.

"Was anyone else hurt?"

Chapman didn't answer.

"Was anyone else—?"

"Yes." His voice was so low she could hardly hear him.

"Who?"

"There's plenty of time to talk about that. Why don't I go hunt you up a smoothie?" He turned to leave.

Something in his voice alarmed her. "Tell me, now. Who else was hurt?"

He hesitated at the door before he returned to the bedside and took her hand.

"The cashier was cut by some glass—nothing serious, just a few stitches on her arm. The owner and a mechanic who was working nearby got a little bruised up. You got the worst of it. Except for Derek Grey."

"Derek? What was he doing there?" She tried to piece it together. "Did he take me there? Is he all right?"

"He's . . . he's dead, Samantha."

She stared at Chapman, trying to comprehend. She had the weird feeling that with the eye bandages removed, she wasn't hearing right. What had he said? Derek was—?

"According to witnesses, while you were paying the bill, he was checking something in your car. There was a big explosion. He was killed instantly."

A dull throb filled her head. Fresh agony overcame her.

"That garage! Those inept mechanics! They killed Derek!" She pounded her fists hard against the mattress. Sharp pain shot through her eyeballs.

"It wasn't ineptitude that killed him, Samantha. Someone planted an explosive device in your car."

"A what? An explo . . . a bomb? That's crazy! Who would put a bomb in my car?"

"It was set on a timer. Presumably you would have driven the car out of the shop and been several blocks away when—"

She raised her hand, a silent plea for him to stop. She couldn't bear to hear more.

Derek! Dead! Her eyes filled with hot tears. Crying made the pain unbearable, but it was nothing compared to the convulsive throes of her grief.

Chapman sat on the bed and held her. "I'm sorry," he whispered. "I shouldn't have told you so soon."

After a while, her sobs subsided. She blotted her eyes and tried to make sense of everything, but the throbbing in her head made it too hard to think.

"This is crazy! Who would want to kill me?"

"We're working on it," Chapman replied. "You have to admit, there are some prime candidates."

The truth of what he said sucked the air from her lungs. She could not imagine it.

"No." Her voice was a hoarse whisper. "That's just too much."

"Think about how well you know De Theret operations," Chapman said. "Probably makes them nervous as hell. That's why I tried to get you to stay away from there."

She considered the plausibility of his words. It could be true. It could be horribly true. She started to tremble.

"What about Lista? Could they have tried to . . . to hurt her, too?"

Chapman did not answer. His expression told her there was more bad news.

"You know something," she guessed. "You know something more about Lista. Where is she?"

"Maybe you should rest for a while. We can talk later."

"Stop treating me like a child. Lista is my friend. I deserve to know what happened to her. I want to know now!"

His eyes revealed the answer before he uttered the words.

"You found her body," she said quietly.

"We did."

"No!" She wailed and shook her pain-wracked head. "No, no, no, no, no!"

She tried to escape the bed, but she was too weak. Grief overtook her, broke her into a million pieces. Chapman held her again, her tears falling on his neck.

Every sadness, every fear she'd held at bay for so long came crashing in. She cried for Lista, she cried for Derek, she cried for her long-gone parents and brother, she cried for Chapman's wife and children, and she cried for her own desolation.

The pain in her eyes and her head grew worse with each sob, but she could not stop. Everything was pain and tears.

A knock at the door of her hospital room roused Samantha from an exhausted stupor.

Poking his head in, a uniformed officer addressed Chapman. "That woman, Gertrude Gold is back. Says she's the lady's secretary?"

Chapman looked to Samantha for the answer. She nodded.

"She's been up here every day," Chapman said, "but we haven't let anyone in to see you. Can she be trusted?"

"Gertie?" The question surprised her. "Of course she can be trusted. She's been my right hand for years."

"Are you absolutely certain?"

"On my life." She shuddered at the irony of her answer.

CHAPTER TWENTY

A Minor Inconvenience

E. B. screamed into the phone. "I said no calls, you idiot!"

In a blind fury, she shoved the phone off her desk. It sailed across the room, followed by papers, files, a cup full of pens and paper clips, and a bud vase with a red silk rose that managed to remain intact upon impact with the littered carpet.

She threw herself onto the empty desk and sobbed.

It wasn't Derek Grey's death that had her grief-stricken. Not at all.

How was it possible that Samantha Newman was still alive?

E.B. sobbed into her folded arms. "That stupid, ugly, useless bih-hitch!" Her plans were ruined, and Samantha Newman had ruined them.

Someone dared to knock on the door.

"Ms. Odom?" A timid voice came through, muffled, but recognizable. Kevin Molton, the little creep. "Ms. Odom?"

She raised her head. "What is it?"

"Ms. Odom?"

"What do you want?"

"Excuse me, Ms. Odom?"

Couldn't he just get on with it? "Speak!"

"Ms. Odom, it's Kevin? I'm sorry to disturb you, but Mr. De Theret wants to know if you could come to his office for a meeting."

"Now?"

"Yes, ma'am. We were supposed to meet to talk abou—"

"Not now. Tomorrow."

"Tomorrow?"

"Yes, tomorrow." Jeez, he was slow.

"Uh, okay. Yes, ma'am. Sorry I bothered you. Oh, uh, you might check your telephone. I couldn't connect to your extension just now. It just rings and rings. So, uh. . . well . . . bye."

At last, he was gone. And yet, however annoying, Molton's brief appearance had presented her with a new perspective.

Her anger evaporated. She sat up, feeling much better. So what if there was a glitch in her plan? All was not lost.

She would probably miss Derek. He was good. Really good. But, like any man, he had been merely a tool to get what she really wanted. Replacing him was only a minor inconvenience. The search for someone new might even be entertaining.

The real sticking point, the bugaboo that would not go away, was Samantha Newman. The woman had been a thorn in her side from the moment they met, with that perfect auburn hair, those naturally straight teeth.

And she was smart. Not that she could hold a candle to E.B. in shrewdness. But why was she so hard to get rid of?

Too much was at stake. Next time, there would be no miscalculation. There was much to do, personal business to settle, and new plans to be made. E.B. grabbed her bag and walked out.

Her assistant tried to hand her a message as she breezed past.

She waved her off. "Save it. I'm gone for the day. By the way, there's a mess in my office. Get somebody to clean it up."

CHAPTER TWENTY-ONE

Pandora's Box

Samantha left the hospital with doctor's orders to stay home for a week of bed rest. Within two days, despite the lingering pain, she was going stir crazy.

She itched to get to the bottom of the explosion that killed Derek. To do that, she had to get back to the office, even though the thought of occupying the same space with E.B. Odom and Vinson De Theret disgusted her.

Carter Chapman called her every morning to make sure she was okay.

"I'm fine. A hundred percent. I'll be back in my office in no time. Then we can work on getting the goods on E.B. and Vinson."

Chapman exploded. "Are you out of your mind? You think you can play nice with these murderers and hope they share their deepest secrets with you?"

"It was your idea to have me expose them from the inside."

"This is not some cops-and-robbers TV show, Samantha. They tried to murder you!"

"I want to do what I can, while I still have a job there."

In the end, Samantha promised to give Chapman and the FBI a few more days to do their work. She was still a little loopy from the pain meds, anyway, and to outsmart Vinson and E.B., she knew she'd need a clear head.

In the meantime, maybe the feds would turn up something concrete. But if, by the end of the week, they weren't ready to pounce, she planned to proceed. She'd been thinking about it since the day she left the hospital.

As the days passed, an idea formed, the seed of a plan that—given the right conditions—might flower. The more she ran it though her mind, the more certain she was.

She would need the help of someone who had come to her aid before, long ago. But first, she had to find him. And she had to make sure that Carter Chapman would not find out.

From her week in the hospital, and the days since she'd been home, he'd been a reassuring presence. Every gesture, how he'd held her when she cried, every touch felt like good medicine. Perhaps he had changed his mind about what he'd read in her old police file. But if he got wind of what she was planning, he might change his mind back again.

Fighting the soreness in her ribcage, she pushed herself out of bed. In the mirror, her bruised body showed few physical marks, but the stiffness in her back and hips was obvious. She still felt like she'd been tossed from a train.

She slipped on the protective goggles she was supposed to wear until her eyes fully healed. They made her look goofy, but while she was at home, she didn't mind.

Her destination was the rear wall of her walk-in closet. She limped a few feet and opened the door. In a back corner, she negotiated the intricacies of lowering her body into a sitting position. She readjusted her goggles, feeling like a deep-sea diver preparing to comb the ocean depths for sunken treasure.

Behind a thick curtain of business suits, she pawed around for the familiar shape of a certain box. When her fingers touched the one with the bumpy studs on top, her pulse quickened. She tugged it toward her and stared at it, unopened in front of her.

Though it resembled a pirate's treasure chest, it held painful reminders of the saddest time in her life. Items she'd never wanted to see again. Yet she'd saved them all these years. Perhaps her younger self somehow knew there would be a time when she would need to face them again, to examine the truths they represented, and to reconcile with the past.

She ran her hands along the top of the box, playing her fingertips across the bumps, remembering. Somewhere inside might be the one thing she needed to work her plan. If she found it, she hoped she had the guts to use it.

Carter Chapman was fully aware that, unless something broke their way soon, he wouldn't be able to stop Samantha from returning to her job.

Time was short, and there were still too many unanswered questions. If Samantha couldn't be controlled, she would have to be protected. He needed to find someone else to work with inside the De Theret organization. But who?

The only person he knew besides Samantha was her secretary, Gertrude Gold. The woman had seemed nice enough when they met her last week at the hospital. But she seemed a bit elderly for undercover work. And yet, she was someone Samantha trusted.

He grabbed his phone. After several clicks, a male voice came on the line.

"This is Kevin Molton. May I help you?"

Chapman was confused. "I thought I called Samantha Newman's office."

"Your name, please?"

"Is this Samantha Newman's office?"

"I am taking her calls," Molton retorted. "Who's calling?"

Chapman was losing patience. "Look, I want to talk to Samantha Newman's secretary. Are you she?"

"Certainly not."

"Then connect me with her. Now!"

The line went silent. Chapman wasn't sure if he had been put on hold or disconnected. He waited, hoping to hear the voice of Gertrude Gold.

"This very rude person insists on talking to you," Molton barked through the intercom. He clicked off.

Gertie picked up the line. "This is Gertrude Gold. May I help you?"

"Mrs. Gold, this is Carter Chapman. I met you last week. Do you remember?"

"Yes, I do." Who could forget such a handsome man? And the way he treated Samantha, so nice. He had seemed like more than a friend.

"I know this may be abrupt, but I don't have much time. I'd like to meet with you today, if possible."

The urgency in his voice puzzled Gertie. What could he want with her? "Today? Okay."

"When can you get away?"

"I take lunch in about an hour."

"Excellent. Do you remember where we met . . . exactly?"

"Exactly?" Gertie's mind returned to the hospital. Samantha had been in room number . . . five twenty-six. That was it.

"Yes," she replied. "I think so."

"See you there in an hour. And please, don't say anything to anyone."

She hung up. Why were they meeting at the hospital, when Samantha was already home? Was she back in the hospital? Why did he say not to tell anyone about their meeting?

She wasn't used to such a cryptic conversation. Before her mind ran away with itself, she dialed

Samantha's number. It took a few rings before she got an answer.

"Gertie! Good to hear from you."

So, Samantha was home. But she seemed out of breath. "Are you okay?"

"Absolutely. Why?"

"You sound a little winded."

"I almost didn't hear the phone. I was digging around in my closet for something, and by the time I heard it ringing, well, I guess I'm not quite ready yet to zip up and down that fast. Whew! How are things at the office?"

"Oh, fine." No use telling her that E.B. was cannibalizing most of her job. Better wait until she was a little stronger. "Nothing to worry about."

"I always knew you'd do great without me."

"We know that's not true," Gertie argued, flattered all the same. "We miss you."

"I'm sure."

"Well, I miss you."

"Thanks Gert. I'll probably be back next week. Do you need me for anything?"

"No, not really." Gertie tried to think of a way to move the conversation toward the real reason for her call. "I, uh, I wanted to ask you . . ."

"Ask me what?"

"Oh, uh, can I, uh, bring you some chicken soup? I'm making it tonight. I can deliver it at lunch tomorrow."

"I'd love some. And I'd love your company. But don't put yourself out for me. Really, I'm okay."

"Speaking of company, has that nice man come by to see you?"

"Man?"

"The one who was with you at the hospital?"

"Oh. Well, yes."

"He seems nice. And so handsome," Gertie pressed. "He's a friend?"

"Friend? I guess so."

"A good friend?"

"Why do you ask?"

"Oh, no reason. He just seems nice, that's all."

"Yes, he does."

"Oh well, I'll see you tomorrow," Gertie said. "Keep getting better."

"Will do. Thanks for calling."

Gertie hung up. At least Samantha sounded okay. But she wasn't very forthcoming about Carter Chapman. So, who was he, really, and what was this meeting about?

CHAPTER TWENTY-TWO

The New V.P.

Kevin Molton floated out of Vinson De Theret's office. Behind his round tortoise-shell spectacles, his eyes were wide with amazement, his face as glazed as a Tussaud waxwork.

Rita Simkin, De Theret's private secretary and gatekeeper, watched Molton as he passed her desk.

Looks like he's seen the face of God, she thought. She wondered if he had been fired.

She hoped so. There were far too many pompous little know-nothings running after her boss these days. Brown-nosing wannabes, each one believing he could run the company someday.

Molton was one of the worst. It sometimes seemed that if Vinson De Theret made a quick turn, the little twerp's nose would break off.

Rita was the only other secretary of a certain age at the company besides Gertrude Gold. It was E.B.'s job to supply Vinson with a competent executive assistant, and she made certain to hire one who couldn't compete in the sex appeal department. Rita may have been a looker in her day, but her wrinkles automatically disqualified her for the Elite Professionals division. Which made her the perfect candidate for the job.

From behind her desk, Rita could only guess at what had sent Molton into a trance. E.B. and De Theret were still inside, and the closed door made it impossible to eavesdrop.

Behind that door, E.B. Odom and Vinson de Theret continued the conversation that had begun with a promotion for Kevin Molton.

De Theret sat behind his desk nursing a scotch. "Do you think we did the right thing?"

E.B. checked her coiffure in the mirror behind the bar. "I know that Kevin's not what Derek could have been for us. He'll never run the South American operation by himself. But with my help, he'll do, for now."

"But what if he starts asking more questions than you want to answer?"

"Kevin is more ambitious than smart. He'll do anything we say, as long as we keep him happy. And that'll be easy enough, with a little more money and a great big new title." She snickered. Kevin Molton, Division Manager, South America. Whatever.

"But it means more work for you. And more exposure."

E.B. turned to face him. "What an old lady you are! Nothing will go wrong. I'll make the first trip with him and introduce him to our contacts. They already know how to handle him."

She sashayed toward him. De Theret's attention followed her progress. As she sat in one of the low-slung chairs across the desk from him, her skirt rode high enough to start one of his blinking spasms.

She pretended not to notice. "Molton thinks the people down there are our business consultants, and that the transports he'll oversee are government requisitions."

"But he's so . . . green. For us to risk everything on so naive a kid—"

"That's what makes him perfect," she countered. "He'll be so excited about his big responsibility and so uptight about doing everything right, he won't have time to question anything. It's even better than having Derek. It's perfect, really."

De Theret peeled his eyes away from her thigh to control the spasms. He gulped his drink and cleared his throat, as if he was gearing up for a long speech.

"Listen, E.B., I want to talk to you about something else."

"Can't we do this later, Vinnie? I've got to get back to my office. I'm really swamped today, now that I'm doing Samantha's job too."

De Theret swiveled his chair halfway toward the window behind him and stared out. "I want to talk about this now."

She recognized the tone. He had something unpleasant on his mind. She waited, not moving so much as a false eyelash.

"You know how much I hate to upset you," he said, "but there's something we have to talk about. I'm sorry, but—"

She bolted up from the chair. "What is it, for Pete's sake? Just spit it out and let me get on with my life!"

Her anger pulled the words out of him. "It's the police. They keep calling and asking more questions. They seem to think somebody tried to kill Samantha, that the explosion that killed Derek wasn't an accident."

He swiveled the chair to face her again. "Now, before you get upset, I know that can't be true. But there's too much going on around here without the cops breathing down my neck."

E.B.'s face was serene. "Kill Derek? Why would anyone want to do that?"

"It was Samantha's car. They think somebody was after her."

"Her car was always blowing up."

"That's what I told the cops. I told them that. I said nobody I knew would want to kill anybody. We needed Derek and Samantha. I told them all that."

"So, what's the problem?"

De Theret's voice was low when he answered. "You kept complaining that she was a problem. You always wanted her out of the way. You were always saying—"

"Stop it. Stop!"

A roaring silence filled the air between them.

E.B. caught her breath. "You don't mean . . . you can't think that I . . ."

Her body quivered all over. She burst into loud, heavy sobs.

De Theret moved toward her and held her heaving shoulders while she whimpered.

"I'm sorry, darling," he whispered. "I'm sorry. I wasn't thinking."

"No, you weren't." She pushed him away.

He tried to pull her back, but she resisted. "Not now, Vinny. I have to get back to my office."

"Darling, forgive me. I—"

She stopped him with a dagger gaze. "No need to apologize. I understand. I know I've said those things about Samantha, but it was only because I was afraid and jealous."

"Jealous?"

She managed to squeeze some waterworks into her eyes. "You must see how she's tried to get close to you. I've been so afraid that you . . . that I might lose you. I want her gone, it's true, but not . . ." She buried her face in his shoulder again.

"Of course not," he said. "I was stupid."

Tears welled at the crimson rims of his eyes. "Why would I want her, when I have you? How could you ever think that? You're my everything, my love, my business, my life. And you always will be."

The tears flowed freely down his cheeks. They dripped into E.B.'s stiffly sprayed hair and glued it to his face.

"Forgive me," he sputtered. "I've been a bad boy again. I should be punished, shouldn't I? I've been so bad, to think that you . . ." His sobs dragged him down to his knees, still clinging to her.

She pulled away and left him teetering. "No. You don't need to be punished. I forgive you. Let's forget it."

"But darling," he pleaded, "I need—"

"I forgive you," she repeated angrily.

"But I—"

"Forget it. I told Kevin I'd meet him for lunch to go over some details. I'm late." She crossed the room and strode out.

CHAPTER TWENTY-THREE

Someone Inside

The fifth floor of Saint Luke's Hospital was alive with noontime activity.

Juggling a flower arrangement from the florist shop downstairs, Gertrude Gold negotiated her way over the damp, freshly mopped linoleum, past the meal carts and medical machines that filled the hallway.

It was silly, buying flowers with no one to give them to, but it felt even sillier coming to the hospital without a sick friend to visit. Carrying the arrangement calmed her a little as she anticipated her clandestine appointment.

She arrived at room 526 and knocked softly. Without waiting for an answer, she opened the door. In the bed Samantha had once occupied lay an elderly man encased head to toe in plaster, contemplating a bowl of uneaten purple Jell-O on the tray before him. He gave Gertie a forlorn look.

"Oh dear. Wrong room. Sorry." She offered an embarrassed smile and retreated to the hallway.

What to do? The room number was right, but Chapman was nowhere to be seen. The bouquet tickled her sinuses. A spate of sneezes overcame her. Her throat began to itch. She looked up and down the corridor. No Chapman.

That does it, she thought. She peered at the patient's name on the door of Room 526 and reentered.

"Mr. Kleschevsky?" Without waiting for acknowledgement, she approached his bed. "Flowers for you." She set the arrangement next to an empty bedpan. "Have a nice day."

Making a hasty exit to the hall, she ran squarely into the strong frame of Carter Chapman.

"Excuse me, Mrs. Gold," he apologized. "Sorry to keep you waiting."

"Oh, that's okay. I was just . . . I was . . . aaahchhzoooo!"

"Bless you."

She rummaged through her purse for a tissue to blow her nose.

"Shall we go down to the cafeteria?" Chapman offered. "We can eat while we talk."

Before she could answer, he guided her purposefully toward the elevator.

The hospital cafeteria was festooned in cheerful hues. Gertie and Chapman got their lunches quickly and found an empty table. As she unwrapped her tuna sandwich, she caught him studying her intently.

His phone beeped. He checked it, put it aside and returned to her. "I wish we had time for a casual chat today, Mrs. Gold, but I'm under tight time constraints. I'm sure you have to get back to the office, too. Forgive me if I get right to the point."

Chewing her sandwich, she nodded. The suspense was killing her. "Go ahead, please."

"What I'm about to tell you may be a bit shocking. I need your assurance that everything we speak of here goes no further than this table. Lives depend on it. Especially Ms. Newman's."

She tried to swallow the wad of sandwich in her mouth. Though she knew next to nothing about Chapman, something told her he was not over-dramatizing.

"Sure," she managed, despite the wad, and the lump of dread rising in her throat.

Chapman leaned in. "I've been working with the FBI to get to the heart of a multi-city crime ring, specifically, a call girl and drug smuggling operation that we're certain is run from the offices of De Theret International. I got as close as I could without cracking the shell, then it became obvious that, without help from someone inside the operation, I would never get enough hard evidence for an indictment. For reasons I won't go into here, I once believed Samantha would be my ace in the hole, but— Am I going too fast?"

Gertie felt her face warming. "Sorry. I wasn't quite expecting . . . Please, continue."

"Which part didn't you get?"

She fanned herself with a napkin. "I think I got it all. It's just that, well, life is full of surprises, isn't it? I had this crazy idea that you wanted to talk to me about something completely different. Silly me."

"Not at all. There's no way you could have expected this. Sorry I've shocked you. If we weren't so short of time—"

"I'm not all that shocked. I work at De Theret International because I love Samantha, and because not many places will hire a woman my age. But I have no fondness for some of the people there. To hear there's something crooked going on doesn't surprise me. I may look like somebody's bubbe, Mr. Chapman, but I wasn't born yesterday. You said Samantha was trying to help you before the accident?"

"Yes. However, it wasn't an accident."

Not an accident? Gertie was speechless. Maybe she *was* too old for this kind of thing. Still, if she could help Samantha . . .. "Go on, please."

"Here's the thing. After I met Ms. Newman, I discovered that, in addition to the crimes I'd been investigating, there's pretty clear evidence that one or more employee deaths can be traced to the De Theret operation. Samantha came very close to becoming the latest victim."

"Deaths? Victim? You mean *murders*?" Gertie swallowed hard. "So, what are you asking me to do? Take Samantha's place? Because I . . . I'd do anything I could, of course—" Her words gave way to a sudden coughing seizure.

She took a gulp of her iced tea, but it only made her choke again. Tears ran down her cheeks. Slowly, she regained control and patted her damp face with a napkin.

"I appreciate the offer, Mrs. Gold," Chapman said, "but, as Samantha's secretary, you are too close to her to do us much good."

"But you need someone you can trust."

"Somebody tried to kill Samantha. If you appear the least bit nosey, you might put yourself in jeopardy, too."

Gertie processed what he'd said, alternating between shock and anger. Anger won. Something had to be done to stop whatever was going on.

"Mr. Chapman, you may have caught me off guard with your story, but I'm too old to scare anymore. If I can help, I will."

"Good. I'm hoping you might know another person at the company. Someone who confides in you, who would not be suspect. A person you could trust to let you know what's going on. Someone with an ear to Vinson De Theret's office, so to speak. It's a shot in the dark, but right now, it's all I have."

She searched her brain. The answer dawned. "I think I can help you."

She leaned closer to him and lowered her voice to a near-whisper. "There is such a person, a relative of mine. Not even Samantha knows this, but the reason I applied for a job at De Theret was because this person told me that Samantha was looking for a secretary and that I'd be perfect for the job. I've never told anyone about having a relative at De Theret, because there's a company policy against it."

Chapman's eyes lit up. "Does this person work closely with De Theret?"

"Close enough to know what's going on, if anybody does."

"Can they be trusted?"

"Blood is thicker than water in my family, Mr. Chapman. None of us would want to work for crooks. Just tell me what you want me to do."

He beamed. "Mrs. Gold, you have made my day."

He has a nice smile, Gertie thought. She chuckled.

"A private joke?" he asked.

"Oh, I was just thinking about how different this meeting turned out to be from what I expected."

He looked puzzled.

"I didn't know why you wanted to talk to me," she explained. "But if I'd had to guess, I would never have thought . . . It's silly, really." She studied him before she decided to share what she'd been thinking.

"Samantha has no family, you know. In truth, I've always felt like a mother to her."

She gave him a little smile. "When you called, I indulged in a little fantasy that maybe you wanted to tell me . . . well, I thought our conversation would be about you and Samantha in a more personal way. Forgive me, it's just that, I noticed how you watched over her in the hospital. I've probably read too many romance novels."

Chapman put a gentle hand on hers. "You're not wrong, Mrs. Gold. But there's unfinished business to deal with before we can think about personal matters."

"I see that, now. It's just that I want her to be happy. She deserves so much more joy than life has offered her." She chuckled. "I was prepared to give you the once over, today. But now you've completely rattled me. I'll do whatever I can to help."

"Good. Tell me more about the person you mentioned. Your relative?"

From Gertie's description, Chapman seemed satisfied that her suggestion was worth trying. He asked for one more favor.

"Samantha doesn't know about this meeting. I'd like to keep it that way. She's got some kind of Wonder Woman image of herself, like she has to singlehandedly fix things. I'm sure she'd be upset if she knew you were helping me."

"I know what you mean, Mr. Chapman. Mum's the word."

Abuzz with anticipation, Gertie hurried back to the De Theret International building. There was work to be done, and someone she needed to see.

CHAPTER TWENTY-FOUR

Coed Confidential

Samantha propped herself up in bed and sifted through the studded box she'd pulled from the depths of her closet. The coverlet was littered with rediscovered relics from her high school and college years.

She'd meant to look straightaway for a certain item, but for most of the morning she'd been lost in remembrance. Slowly and tenderly, layer by layer, the few concrete remnants of her past were laid bare. Some brought her squarely up against the worst memories. Like the box that held them, she'd kept them buried deep.

It was two weeks into her freshman year at college when the Office of the Dean called her in. The replay of that meeting could still knock her to the ground.

"I have some very bad news, Miss Newman," the woman had said. "I'm sorry to have to tell you this. I received a phone call a little while ago from the police in your hometown. It seems that last night there was a fire at your parents' house. Unfortunately, they were asleep and unaware of the smoke. Your brother tried to drag them out, but in the end, all three were overtaken. No one survived."

She did not remember much of what the Dean said after that, but from that day on, the sad facts of the incident were part of her life story. An electrical short. A tragic accident. Nobody's fault.

Now, proof of her desolation was reduced to the mementos that lay before her: a stack of condolence cards, three entries in the hometown obit column, newspaper clippings about the fire—complete with photos of the burned-out home—and the last communication she had from her family.

On the reverse side of a snapshot of the four of them, taken the day she left for school, a short note was written in her mother's rounded script.

Have a good year, darling. Don't forget what we look like! And remember, we love you.

Samantha stared at the photo, studying every familiar detail. When her eyes were too full to see, she slipped it into the pocket of her robe and reached for a tissue. Goggles off, she let her tears flow. No use holding back now.

After a while, the tears subsided. She couldn't remember why she had shut the picture away with the other things. Maybe it had hurt too much to look at back then. Now, it comforted her to remember what it was like to have a family.

She wiped her cheeks, blew her nose, and readjusted the goggles.

Next out of the box came photo albums from her childhood. Then, her high school yearbooks. She suppressed the urge to browse through them and set them aside.

Something was stuck to the front of her college yearbook. She peeled off the narrow, slightly curled paper and turned it over. It was a photo strip of two young women making funny faces at the camera. Her heart stopped as the memory flooded in.

First day of college. She and Lista had just met, in the dorm room they were assigned to share. They decided to check out a sorority party that night. Though the party was a bust, the cheesy photo-booth memento had recorded the moment they bonded. Two college girls on their own for the first time, their whole lives ahead of them, celebrating. That was before the fire, and before, well. . . everything else.

She reached for another tissue. Through a blur of fresh tears, she studied the girls' goofy expressions, so full of lighthearted fun, freedom, and endless possibilities. It was hard to remember what that felt like. But one thing was certain. When all this was over, she wanted to feel those things again.

She stuck the photo strip into her pocket next to the one of her family and blotted her eyes. There would be time, later, to revisit the life they had shared, to mourn the losses, and rejoice at the memories. Something more urgent was pressing her to move on.

Peering into the half-empty box, she spotted a small stack of business cards that were barely held together by a fraying rubber band. Her pulse quickened as she sorted through them, looking for the one she needed. There was a card from the Office of the Dean, another from her hometown police department, another from the fire department, one from the funeral home, a few from take-out restaurants, a bank, and one from Derek's old law practice.

Her mind rewound as she stared at Derek's card. It represented another chapter in her life she'd never planned to revisit. Was it really necessary to conjure up those memories?

Lista and Derek were her saviors, back then. He was the fresh-out-of-law-school attorney who had helped her through the struggles she'd faced after her family died. And poor, lost Lista. She was the first person to reach out after the tragedy. Both of them, gone. Who else would stand up for them now?

She was down to the last card. It was the one she'd been searching for, and dreaded to find. She should have tossed it years ago, like a piece of toxic waste. In the wrong hands, it could cause her endless embarrassment and harm.

But today, it could hold the answer to her prayers. This wasn't the time to worry about protecting herself. She had a plan and believed it would work. It had to.

Making this call would be the first step. She wondered if the number was still good. Her heart pounded and her hands trembled as she picked up the phone.

"Angel's Coed Confidential," a young female voice answered. "This is Melody. May I help you?"

Samantha's heart flipped. "Melody?" Though it shouldn't have, the name took her by surprise.

"Yes," the sweet voice answered. "May I help you?"

"I need to speak with the Angel, please."

"Angel?"

"Yes. This is Samantha Newman. I . . . I used to work for him, a long time ago. I'm calling long distance. I need to talk to him."

"The Angel doesn't usually—"

"Please, it's very important. He can call me back, if he wants. Tell him . . . tell him there's no trouble. I just need him to verify employment for me."

"Verify employment?" Melody sounded even more doubtful.

"I'll explain when I talk to him. No hassle, I promise."

"What was your name again?"

"Samantha Newman. I'm sure he'll remember me, but in case he doesn't, tell him . . . remind him I used to be Melody."

"Melody? Like me?"

"Yes. I was Melody, a long time ago."

"Well, I guess I could give him the message."

"Thank you. Please tell him that it's urgent. I'll be at this number all day."

The girl on the phone promised she would do her best.

Samantha hung up, buzzing with adrenaline. Too agitated to stay in bed, she grabbed the old albums and yearbooks and padded her way downstairs to make some tea and wait for the Angel to return her call.

Her entire plan depended on his cooperation. He had come through for her once before, but that was a long time ago. Now she could only wait and hope that he would do it again.

CHAPTER TWENTY-FIVE

Fra Diablo

E.B. Odom and Kevin Molton had just ordered lunch. The noise level at Carrabba's was higher than usual, mostly from the raucous bachelorette party at the next table.

E.B. jiggled the ice in her glass of bourbon. "You've got a lot to learn in a very short time, Kevin."

"I know." He was eager to prove to her and De Theret that he could handle any job they gave him. "I promise I can do it. I'm a really fast learner."

"That's good." She stroked the condensation off her water glass with her fingertips. "I like a fast learner."

"That's me."

He hoped she wouldn't notice the perspiration he felt on his upper lip. His eyeglasses threatened to slip down his nose. He caught them just in time and pushed them up again.

Mercifully, she had been concentrating on her phone, reading a text message. He blotted his lip and waited patiently. Best not to annoy her.

When she caught Molton looking at her, E.B. shut the phone and turned her amber eyes to him, locking him in her gaze.

"It's good that you're up for the challenge, Kevin."

He was uncomfortable around E.B., but he needed to impress her. To please E.B. was to please Vinson De Theret. The promotion meant that he'd succeeded, he guessed. He just needed to make sure not to blow it.

Molton had never really dealt with E.B. one-on-one like this, away from the office. The prospect of finding his footing as director of the South American division made him less anxious than the idea of working closely with her.

"I hope you're pleased with your new position." She stroked his hand.

Startled, he jerked his hand away before it dawned on him that the gesture had been intentional. "Sorry. I didn't mean to—?"

"No problem. But you should understand that we'll be working very closely together. No need to keep your distance."

Her directness made him blush. He took a long swig of the bourbon E.B. had ordered for him, too.

Her eyes were still on him as he struggled to swallow. "You seemed a little hesitant this morning when Vinnie and I offered the job to you."

"I was shocked!" He winced and desperately searched for something smarter to say. If only she wouldn't look at him like that. "Well, not shocked, I guess, but . . . surprised, you know? I mean, South America!" His earlobes tingled.

"Why would you be surprised, Kevin? You've done a good job in the training department and the other little assignments we've given you along the way. You've shown loyalty, and that's what's important. We're rewarding you for a job well done."

Her eyes narrowed. "Aren't you ready for success?"

"Are you kidding?" He tried to sound confident. "Of course I'm ready. It's just that I didn't expect it." Uh-oh.

He hadn't meant to say that. "I mean, I didn't expect it would be this job. I thought I'd maybe have Samantha Newman's job one day. This is better than I hoped for."

E.B. stared at him for what seemed like a century.

He couldn't think of anything more to say. Probably said too much already. Was she angry, or what? He waited for the chips to fall.

Her eyes narrowed to slits, and she chuckled. At least he thought it was a chuckle. It was an odd sound, almost like a rattle.

She burst into contained, silent laughter that wracked her shapely figure. A scarlet tinge spread from the deep V of her blouse up to her milk-white neck.

His eyes followed the progress of the blush, then returned to the heaving cleft from whence it came. He forced himself to look away.

Her hand touched his chin and lifted his gaze to hers. Her other hand grasped his.

"I'm sorry if I . . ." he began helplessly.

"Don't apologize." She stroked his hand with her long fingertips. "Don't ever be sorry for being ambitious. I like that about you, Kevin."

"You do?" He ventured a direct look at her, trying to read what she meant.

"Yes, I do. And I like your idea."

"My idea?" His face was hot again.

"Your idea about taking Samantha Newman's job."

"But . . . what about . . . what about . . ." He was stricken with the fear that he'd just jeopardized his new promotion. "I didn't mean, I mean, I . . ."

She pressed her diamond-tipped index finger to his lips. "There's no need to explain. I understand perfectly. It's important that you share your fantasies with me. If you do everything I need you to do for me now, you could be in charge of . . . whatever it is Ms. Newman was . . . is in charge of."

He was speechless.

E. B. didn't seem to notice. "Now then, let's talk about the next few days."

He was grateful for a change of subject. Feeling more secure, he picked up the conversation.

"I'll be working with Allison Winslow this afternoon to get her ready to take over my training classes."

E.B. frowned. "Allison Winslow? Isn't she that little goody-goody blonde from Kansas?"

"Ohio."

"Whatever. She doesn't seem strong enough to motivate the trainees."

"She's been leading half the training classes while I've worked in Ms. Newman's office. And she's done a great job. Plus, she's been a top producer every month for the last six months."

"I know that," E.B. said. "I just don't think she really fits in, long term. What about that good-looking young man I interviewed last month? The one I sent down to you?"

"Evan Farrell?"

"That's the one."

Molton studied E.B.'s expression for a hint that she was joking. She was not. "But Evan hasn't finished his own training! He barely knows how to find the men's room. He—"

"That's enough," she hissed. "I happen to know that Evan is going to close a big deal. He's going to be huge for us, really, and he's got the right look for the company. I want to give him some encouragement."

Molton knew that Farrell's first deal was a fluke, beginner's luck that had somehow put the right guy's resume into Farrell's hands on his first day at the job. But he also knew better than to argue with his boss.

"What will I say to Allison?" he moaned. "I told her I had something important to discuss with her after lunch."

"Say that you want to thank her for the good job she's done," E.B. replied coolly, "and that you think she'll make a great trainer someday. Then tell her to get Evan ready for his new job. After that, she can return to her client account rep duties. After all, she can make more money as a headhunter on commission than she ever could being a trainer. You wouldn't want to take that away from her, would you?"

What was he supposed to say? "You want me to talk to Evan this afternoon, too?"

E.B. smiled. "I'll take care of him. And in the future, if you think he needs more help, just send him to me. I'm happy to make sure he knows what he's doing."

Wrung out and more confused than ever, Kevin Molton took a deep breath. He had really, really wanted this lunch to go smoothly, to show he was capable of being the executive he was expected to be. Instead, he had wrangled with his boss, even though he hadn't meant to.

E.B. took his hand and stroked his fingers again. "Don't worry. Sometimes these little things have to be ironed out. Now we can talk about your new future."

"I . . . I'm looking forward to that," he said. "I don't know much about what this job entails."

"I'll teach you everything you need to know, Kevin," she said. "As long as you work closely with me, you'll be fine. I only need to be sure that you are one hundred per cent mine."

He thought he felt his napkin slip and reached to grab it. Instead, he caught E.B.'s hand, resting on his lap. He drew back, startled.

She giggled. "I didn't mean to frighten you. I just want you to know how committed I am to your personal happiness."

Her hand remained where it was. He hoped she wouldn't notice his involuntarily reaction to her touch.

"I . . . I'm . . . grateful," he mumbled.

The waiter arrived with their lunch. Molton stared at the special of the day, his Flounder Fra Diablo. It had sounded good when he ordered it, but now he feared it would be very hard to swallow.

CHAPTER TWENTY-SIX

The Angel

Samantha stood at the cooktop stirring the last of Gertie's chicken soup. She checked the clock. It was almost seven. A day and a half had passed since she'd left her message, but Angelo "The Angel" Infante had not called.

She adjusted her protective eyewear and stared at the silent phone. She'd spent the better part of the day willing it to ring. Each time she checked the clock, her anxiety escalated.

Maybe the girl she spoke to was too frightened to give the message to him. Samantha remembered that when she worked for him, there were strict orders not to bother him with calls from people he didn't know. She'd rather have died than face his wrath for breaking one of his rules. Did this girl feel the same?

Her old high school yearbooks and the photo albums were on the counter. She opened the annual from her senior year to leaf through while she stirred the soup. Silly rhymes and grinning faces of long-forgotten classmates filled the pages. She tried to remember what life felt like back then, before that world disappeared forever.

The phone thundered to life. It made her jump, which sent the soup spoon flying. Hot soup splashed over the open yearbook and soaked into her robe.

Searing heat soaked through her sleeve to her wrist. She grabbed a towel with one hand and the phone with the other.

"Hello?"

"Everything okay?"

It was Carter Chapman. She blotted her sleeve, and the yearbook. "Of course."

"You don't seem happy to hear from me."

"Nothing personal. I'm just not good at sitting around all day."

"It's a tough job, but somebody has to do it. And it's your job this week, until the doc says otherwise. Hey, is this the cranky side of you I'm getting to know?"

"I suppose I am cranky today."

He was doing it again, calming her down, making her smile.

"Listen," he said, "I hear that Asian food works wonders on cranky people. Why don't I pick some up and come over?"

She glanced at the soup, still simmering on the stove. She'd had it for lunch already, and with almost half of it coating everything on the counter, it didn't look too appetizing. She checked the clock again.

It didn't seem like Angelo would be calling, at least not today, and maybe never. Without his help, she had no alternate plan. Then everything would depend on the FBI investigation.

For a lot of reasons, Asian with Chapman sounded pretty good. "Come if you can stand it. But there's a boatload of cranky happening here."

"I can handle whatever you throw at me. See you in an hour."

She hung up, smiling. If only the two of them could get beyond all the awfulness . . .

Maybe he would have positive news. And if not, the Angel might still call tomorrow.

White paper takeout cartons littered the kitchen table. Samantha pushed her plate away. "I can't eat another bite."

Chapman plunged his chopsticks into a carton and came up with an egg roll. He waggled it in front of her. "Last one."

She contemplated the delectable tidbit roll through her goggles. "You eat it."

"Not when I know how much pleasure it brings you. C'mon."

"Oh, well, maybe one more." She grabbed the eggroll and took a bite.

"Atta girl. I knew you could do it."

He carried his plate to the sink and checked the bag on the counter. "How 'bout one of these?"

He held up a fortune cookie. "Lotto number inside, could be your lucky day."

She waved him off. The kitchen phone rang.

She froze. Bits of egg roll formed a giant clump in her mouth. She tried to swallow, but none of it would budge. Was the Angel calling her now?

Another ring.

"Aren't you going to answer?" Chapman asked.

She tried again to swallow. The phone rang a third time.

Another swallow, and the clump moved enough for her to speak. "I'll get it."

Too late. The answering machine picked up.

"The Angel returning your call," a gruff voice announced through the speaker. "You know where to find me."

Chapman looked at her. A question formed on his face.

"Wrong number," she bluffed. "Happens a lot."

He turned to the sink to rinse his plate, but midway through, he shut the water off. "You know this guy."

She held her breath.

"You know this guy," he repeated. He dried his hands and turned to her. "Angel is his name."

"Know him? Why should I know him?" She feigned indifference and dug into a carton of rice with her chopsticks.

"You shouldn't, but you do." Something in his voice chilled her.

She sat paralyzed, hoping he couldn't read her eyes behind the protective glasses. She shoveled more rice into her bowl, though she had no intention of eating it.

"Look," he said, "we haven't talked about it yet, but now's as good a time as any."

"Talk about what?"

"Before our first meeting, I pored over all the information I could find on you."

"I know." She also knew what was coming next. She made circles in the rice with her chopsticks and waited.

"Part of that information had to do with a certain prostitution case. You were a witness for the defense of Angelo 'The Angel' Infante."

"So?" Her heart was pumping full throttle.

"His attorney was Derek Grey. Your testimony helped get Infante off the hook."

"What's wrong with that?"

"Angelo Infante is a known pimp. A pimp, Samantha."

Chapman's tone carried an accusation that was hard to bear. Hands on hips, he waited, for her to respond.

"So, you think that makes me a—"

"Don't say it!"

"Why? Does saying it make it true? Does thinking it make it true? Because that's what you think, isn't it?

"Not anymore."

"Not. . . anymore?" Hot tears filled her eyes.

"I mean, I don't think it anymore. Not since I met you. That's why I was such an oaf to begin with. I'd studied the file on you, and I thought I had you pegged, until we met. Then nothing fit the profile I'd put together."

"My file?" She jammed the chopsticks hard into her bowl, sending rice flying. "What else did my file tell you? Did it tell you my family was wiped out in the blink of an eye" Or that I was left with nothing, no one, and no interest in whether I lived or died? Did it tell you that if it hadn't been for Lista and Derek, and Angelo Infante, I probably wouldn't have survived?"

Her rage filled the breathing space between them as her words echoed around the kitchen.

Chapman looked like he'd been smacked with a wrecking ball. "Guessing was all I had to go on, Samantha. And I guessed wrong."

"Big time!" Eyes blazing behind her goggles, she stood and turned away.

"Please," he said softly. "Tell me the parts that aren't in your file. I want to understand."

He sounded genuinely distraught. Perhaps his theory was understandable, given the information he had. Maybe he deserved an explanation. Just like she deserved a chance to set the record straight.

She turned to face him, but the sadness in his eyes was too much. She took a breath and returned to her chair. Lowering her eyes to the rice-strewn table, she began.

"You know that Lista was my freshman roommate. She worked for the Angel. Yes, as one of those terrible people. Her family was poor as dirt. She put herself through college that way.

"We'd just moved into the same dorm room, barely knew one another. Even so, after my folks died, she supported me out of her own money for the rest of that semester. Tuition, food, clothes, the works. And when I refused to take any more from her, she went to Angelo for help.

"Angelo Infante. Another terrible person, according to you. He gave me a job. Did my file at least tell you what the job was?"

"A receptionist, I think it said."

"And that's what I was. That's all I was."

"But, didn't you know what kind of business . . ."

In his struggle to understand, he pinpointed the crux of the dilemma she'd wrestled with for years. It was time to resolve it. She looked up at Chapman.

"I did, and I didn't. After the fire, I was in such a fog of grief and anger, I don't think I was fully conscious of anything. Mostly, I didn't care. I sat in a cubicle and answered the telephone. If the caller wanted an escort, a model, a babysitter, I'd connect them to somebody else to make the arrangements. That's all I did."

His eyes held more questions. "When Infante was indicted, you didn't have to testify. Didn't you realize—"

She leaned against the chair's back and spoke to the ceiling. "Please, can we stop now?"

"I want to know, Samantha. Why did you testify for him?"

It was no use. Might as well rip off the whole scab.

"When the Angel was arrested, I knew I should feel ashamed. But what I'd been doing was surviving. He paid me three times what I could've made anywhere else working part-time like I did. He made sure my hours were flexible so I could attend all my classes. I stayed in school, supported myself and graduated on-time because of him."

"So that's why you testified?"

"He made it clear I owed him nothing. I knew he was a little shady, and he was a tough boss. But with me, he was a complete gentleman. He went above and beyond to help, just out of the goodness of his heart. I was a character witness for him. I returned the favor."

Her eyes were moist inside the goggles. "I'm not proud of any of it, but it's part of my past, and I can't change it. Sorry to disappoint you."

There were no more questions in Chapman's eyes, only sadness. He turned away and stared out the window.

She watched his back, wondering what he thought of her now. Was it possible he could understand how young and alone she had been back then? How lost?

He was the first to break the silence. "He said he was returning your call."

"What?"

"Angelo Infante. He was returning your call. That means you called him first."

She said nothing.

He turned to face her. "What's going on? Why are you calling him?"

Without her answer, he guessed. "It has something to do with De Theret, doesn't it?"

Again, she did not respond.

"You don't have to tell me," he said. "I know it does. I thought we agreed that you would stay clear of this and let me handle it."

"I will, until the end of the week. That was the agreement."

He shook his head. "I never should have gotten you involved."

"I got myself involved, remember? I sent the message that started this. Besides, you said things could be sewed up by Friday."

"Looks like it might take a little longer."

"What am I supposed to do in the meantime? Dig a hole and hide? While I still have a job, I can use it to help."

"Somebody wants you dead, Samantha. Have you forgotten that?"

"Look, I agreed to wait until Friday, and Friday it is. I'm tired of arguing."

"So am I." Chapman tossed the dish towel into the sink and walked out.

She heard the front door close.

Dirty dishes, spilled rice and open food cartons testified to the evening's unfinished business. She rose and began to clear the rest away.

While she worked, she reconsidered her options. She could back off and give Chapman more time. It was likely that Angelo would wait for her to call him again, so there was no rush. If it all worked out, so much the better.

But what if next week the FBI still wasn't ready, or the week after that, or longer? She'd be living in limbo. How long could she wait?

Years ago, she'd promised herself never to leave her fate to chance again. She had chosen poorly at first, but now there was only one path.

She dried her hands and climbed the stairs to retrieve the number she'd left on her nightstand. Two minutes later, she was calling the Angel.

CHAPTER TWENTY-SEVEN

Nobodies

E.B. Odom lolled beside Vinson De Theret on the sofa in his office, a tall glass of whiskey in her hand.

"You're very quiet tonight, Vinnie. Cat got your tongue?"

Nursing his third scotch, De Theret watched the television news in silence.

She moved closer and whispered his ear. "Has the lil' ol' kitty-cat got your tongue? I'm jealous."

He leaned away from her. A blinking spasm overran his face.

Undaunted, she nuzzled his neck. "Have you been a bad boy?"

"Stop it!" He escaped to the bar to get more ice.

She studied him as he refilled his tumbler with scotch and took a big swallow. The signs were clear. Something unpleasant was on his mind.

She met his gaze with a smile. "What is it, Vinnie? Tell me and I'll fix it, like I always do."

He chugged the scotch from his glass and refilled it. "I think we need to shut down."

She wasn't sure she'd heard him right. "What?"

"Shut down. Close shop. It's time."

She sat up and reached for the remote to click the sound off. Silence fell like lead.

"Did I hear you say, 'shut down'?"

With his back to her, his reply was barely audible. "Yes."

"Shut down what?"

"The side operations."

"Side operations? Which ones?"

He turned to face her. "All of them."

She stared at him, incredulous. "Why?"

"You know why. It's getting too risky."

So that's what had him in a funk. He was afraid of those blasted cops snooping around. His anxiety level was out of control. She should have seen it coming. Better take care of it, now.

She set her drink down and patted her hair in place. "Darling, I see that you're a teensy bit upset. Why shut down, after everything we've worked for? Think about the money. You want to pull the plug on all that money?"

"It's much too dangerous. "The cops—"

She rose and crossed the room, pleading her case as she closed the distance between them. "We're too smart for the cops, Vinnie. I've made sure of that." She reached for his hand.

De Theret brushed it away. "I mean it, E.B."

She slapped him, hard. "*You* mean it? Really? I got news for you."

She stormed away, continuing her tirade as she paced the room. "*I'm* the one who built those operations. I created a friggin' money machine. And now you say you don't want it anymore? You wanna be poor like we used to be? Nobodies, like we used to be?"

Her voice grew hoarse. When breathy spaces replaced most of her words, she collapsed on the sofa.

De Theret sat beside her and took her hand. "Hear me out, please."

When she didn't protest, he continued. "I know how much you mean to the operation, and how much it means to you. But it's *my* name on the business. I say when we close shop."

E.B. sat up. "But—"

"It's time. The deals were beautiful, gorgeous, clean deals when we started. And safe. We could run Elite Professionals out of a shoebox and rake in the dough."

"We did, didn't we?"

To his relief, she seemed to be abandoning her opposition to his plan. "Yeah, we did."

He squeezed her hand. "A handful of satisfied customers, great word-of-mouth, and we were in business. It was simple then. Clean. You had a great idea, and it worked. And you were right about the South American operation. It was the perfect value-added service. And it kept your husband away. Poor dope didn't even know what he was doing for us."

She laughed, a ragged sort of snicker. "Trey used to say, 'I don't understand why I have to babysit everything between here and there. Why don't we just ship the files?' And I'd say, 'Vinson trusts you. It's all good.' He said he felt like a bag man for the Mafia."

De Theret chuckled. "He loved you." His grin faded. "But then, when his plane exploded, and—"

"Stop!" She covered her ears. "I don't need a stroll down Memory Lane. His plane crashed. So what? Lucky for us!"

"Unlucky for him," De Theret said solemnly. His blinking started up again. He returned to the bar to refresh his drink. "And then in New Orleans, that thing with Lista Pearson . . ."

E.B. stifled a groan. "Lista? Good grief, Vinnie, that girl was always doing stupid things. She had a knack for upsetting people, and she messed with the wrong guy. I didn't have anything to do with that."

She dabbed at her eyes, though there were no tears. "You don't think I killed her, do you?"

"Of course not. But Samantha's car, and Derek. . ."

"Not that again, please." She grabbed her bourbon from the coffee table and took a gulp.

"It's just that it was another explosion, like Trey's plane." His words hung in the air, a floating accusation.

She popped off the sofa. "What do you think I am, Vinnie, a . . . a terrorist? You know me better than that."

De Theret watched her pacing the carpet in front of him. "Whatever caused these . . . mishaps . . . they've brought too much attention on us and the business. We can't afford to operate like this anymore."

"But Vinnie—"

"And another thing. To trust South America to a green bean like Kevin Molton . . . It just isn't safe."

She stopped pacing and turned to him, hands on hips. "I told you, I can handle him. He's so grateful for his new big title, he'll do anything I say. Things aren't so bad. We're still in control."

"It's too risky. I'm pulling us out."

"What about the employees and the clients?"

"They'll find new connections."

"Yeah, and make somebody else rich. I won't do it, Vinnie. I can't let all this go. You call it your deal, but it's mine, too. It was my idea and my work that made it happen. I'll pay you back what it cost you to start it, plus interest. It's too good a deal to let go of. It's—"

"Over. It's over. I expect you to handle the details of closing it all down. End of discussion." He left the sofa to get more ice.

While he was occupied, E.B. walked to a far window. She reached into her blouse to extract her phone, tapped a short message, then returned the phone to its nesting place.

She turned her attention to De Theret. "Pour me another, please."

As he dispensed the liquor, she strolled to the bar, smiling. She clinked her glass against his. "All right, Vinnie. Have it your way."

CHAPTER TWENTY-EIGHT

Half True

Samantha squinted into the sunlight as Chapman steered the Jag into the parking lot for the car rental.

"I give up," she said. How *do* you catch a unique rabbit?"

He came to a stop. "You 'neak up on him."

She stifled a smile.

"Get it?" he prodded. "U-nique. You. 'Neak. You 'neak up on. . . oh, you did get it. You just didn't think it was funny." He made a sad face.

"Well, it was cute," she offered.

"Cute?"

"Cute. Like you."

"Cute. I suppose there are worse things."

Chapman's silly joke helped dispel any left-over tension from their argument in her kitchen three days ago. She suppressed the urge to touch him and grabbed her purse. Best to focus on her plan right now.

He pulled up to the door of the rental office. "Are you sure you're ready to drive?"

"I'm fine. Besides, you have better things to do than cart me around all the time."

Chapman left to park his car. Before he got back to the office, he saw Samantha walking out.

She waved her receipt. "That had to be a world record for fastest time to rent a car. They've got their rapid check-in down to sixty-seconds."

Chapman looked at his watch. "Maybe under a minute. Definitely a record. What kind of car did you get?"

She laughed. "I don't know! When I called, I said I'd take anything. The guy behind the counter was so quick, it was over before I thought to ask."

He gave her a sideways glance.

"Maybe that was a mistake?"

He took her hand. "Let's go see."

They meandered through an acre of cars before they found hers.

Chapman stood beside it, considering. "Well, you did tell them you'd take anything."

"It's a shoebox."

"Definitely not a Corvette. But it is red."

"A red shoebox."

"Well, actually, it's . . . it's kind of—"

"Come on," she teased. "Kind of what?"

"Cute!" He grinned. "Definitely cute."

"In that case, I suppose it was meant to be." She unlocked the door and got in, then lowered the driver's window and offered her hand. "Thank you, for everything."

He leaned down and touched her cheek. She wanted to get out of the car and hug him, just to feel him hold her again, like he had in the hospital. Instead, she took his hand and squeezed it gently.

It felt like they were human magnets, alternately flipping the positive and negative sides, pulling closer, then pushing apart. Would they eventually land on the right side together? She pulled her hand inside and started the car.

He backed off to give her room to pull the car out. "Let me know what the doctor says."

"Okay." She put the car in gear and drove away.

Chapman watched the little red rental exit the lot. Samantha was on her own again. He couldn't shake the feeling that, given half a chance, she'd put herself in harm's way. He had to act fast.

He sat in his car and called Mack Maginnis. "Did we get clearance on the new inside person?"

"Yep," Maginnis said. "Looks clean."

"So, we're finally a go?"

"I guess so."

Something in the agent's tone alarmed him. "You don't sound certain."

"Like I told you before, buddy, there's a lot of room for error here. I mean, you're talking about using somebody who's never done this kind of thing."

"We have to move on this now."

"We're moving on it. These things take time. Our new contact will be coming in later today for prep work. You can assess the situation yourself. By the way, how's your lady friend?"

"She's about to be released by her doctor, and she's hell-bent on going back to work."

"That's not good. We can't protect her there."

"I've warned her, but she doesn't seem to care. Until this thing is over, I'll stay in close contact, as much as possible."

"From what you've told me, that shouldn't be too tough for you."

Tougher than it looks, Chapman thought. "See you back at the bureau."

He got in his car and sat for a moment, staring out the window. Samantha Newman wouldn't sit idle for long, but exactly what she planned to do remained a mystery. She was stubborn as all get-out, and he was helpless to stop her. Unless he could move first.

He pounded the dashboard. Nothing had turned out the way he'd intended, and now there was even more at stake. If only the wheels of justice didn't grind so blasted slowly.

Samantha left the doctor's office feeling strong. She had a clear goal, and she was determined to see it through.

When she got home, she called Chapman.

"I'm free and clear. No goggles, no pain meds, no restrictions."

"Great." He seemed less relieved than she was. "What did the doc say about going back to work?"

"She gave me a full release. Anything I feel like doing."

She expected him to say something, but he didn't protest. Maybe he'd given up.

Still, she offered him a slight concession. "I don't plan to return to my job again, by the way."

Someone was talking to Chapman in the background. She wished she could make out what they were saying.

"Sorry," he said when he returned to the conversation. "We're at a critical juncture here. I didn't get that last thing you said."

She repeated her statement.

"You're not going back to De Theret? That's good news. You made the right decision."

Samantha hesitated. Technically, she hadn't lied to him. She had no intention of returning to her old job. But what he'd understood was only half true. If she told him more, he would only try to stop her.

"Just a sec, Sam." He covered the phone and briefly spoke to someone nearby before he returned to her. "Hey, I gotta go. Let's celebrate your new freedom. I'm working late today, but how about tomorrow? We could drive to my place, if you're up to it."

A weekend at home, alone, stewing over what lay ahead, or one with him at his beautiful country place. Another push, another pull.

It would be hard to keep Carter Chapman at bay for the next few days anyway. What the heck. "Okay."

"Talk to you tomorrow."

She hung up and considered her next move. Chapman would have told her if the case had been resolved at his end, but he didn't. With a clean bill of health from the doctor, there were no more impediments. She had to move forward with her plan, even though it was risky.

She wasn't afraid. In fact, she was exhilarated. She picked up the phone and dialed De Theret International.

The throaty voice of Rita Simkin answered. "Vinson De Theret's office. May I help you?"

"Rita, this is Samantha Newman."

"Ms. Newman! How are you?"

"I'm fine."

"All healed from the accident?"

"Pretty much."

"Will you be returning to us soon?"

"Well, first I'd like to meet with Vinson privately. How does Monday look for him?"

"Hmm. Eleven-thirty is open."

"I'll be there."

CHAPTER TWENTY-NINE

Undercover Stuff

Kevin Molton checked his watch as he ran the last quarter mile of his lunchtime jog. In less than twenty-four hours, he would be on his way to Colombia with E.B. Odom. He was beyond nervous.

He attempted to repeat the phrase that piped through his earphones. "Donday estay la porta?"

His voice was shaky, and not just from pounding down the sidewalk. For days, he'd had trouble breathing normally. His heart seemed to have taken up residence at the top of his esophagus and wouldn't budge, no matter how much deep breathing he attempted.

A recurring image from last night's dream still haunted him.

There was E.B., naked in bed. Instead of fingernails, foot-long spikes sprang from her fingertips. They glinted ominously, reflecting the glare that surrounded her. He was there, too, full of confliction. Should he give in and risk the spikes and the blinding light? Her desire for him seemed overwhelming. He awoke soaked in sweat.

Whenever she discussed their trip to South America, the innuendo was unmistakable. What kind of game was she playing? With E.B., you could never tell.

This was the chance to prove that he really could be somebody, a chance to make a name for himself and earn the respect of important people. The opportunity of a lifetime. He didn't want to blow it.

He rounded the corner and headed back toward the De Theret International Building. "Donday estay la porta," he repeated as he neared the entrance.

He was adjusting the volume control when he nearly collided with Gertrude Gold and Rita Simkin.

"Pardonaymay," he mumbled, sucking air. "Sorry." He retreated inside the lobby.

The two women collected themselves and continued toward their favorite lunch place.

"He has a nice physique, don't you think?" Gertie commented as they walked.

Rita made a face. "That nitwit? He's such a twit, I hadn't noticed. He's as bad as the rest of them, that whole group of self-centered, over-ambitious cannibals."

"Oyoyoy! Sounds like you've had a bad morning."

"I live for the day when E.B. and her little crew of zeroes get their comeuppance. She's ruining De Theret, if you ask me."

Gertie quickly looked around. "This isn't the place to talk. Let's get to the cafe."

"Sorry. I've had about all I can take from that woman."

On the way, Rita told Gertie what had transpired that morning. They were still talking about it over lunch.

While she munched her Greek salad, Gertie tried to make sense of the news Rita had shared. "I wonder what Samantha wants to see Mr. De Theret about."

Rita made a face. "Ms. Odom would sure like to know."

"She really had a hissy fit?"

"Unbelievable! She blew a gasket when she saw Ms. Newman's name on Mr. De Theret's appointment calendar. First, she started grilling me, then she stormed into Mr. De Theret's office, ready to kill. With the door shut, I couldn't hear anything, but she didn't look any happier when she stormed out again. She marched past my desk, muttering. Made my hair stand on end. Thank goodness she'll be out of town when Ms. Newman comes in."

Gertie sat up. "Out of town? Where to?"

"Oh, she's taking that idiot Molton with her to South America. They've promoted him to Derek Grey's . . . uh, you know, Trey Odom's old job. Talk about sending a boy to do a man's work! Anyway, they'll both be out of the office until Tuesday."

Gertie frowned. "What did Mr. De Theret do after Ms. Odom left?"

"I don't know," Rita confessed. "He just stayed in his office, quiet as a mouse. You know, I've worked for that man for over five years and I've seen him get richer and richer. But I swear, sometimes I think he has absolutely no balls."

"Ms. Odom has enough for the two of them," Gertie observed with a grin.

Rita blushed. "Such language from the two of us!"

They giggled.

Gertie lowered her voice. "I'd like to know what goes on with Ms. Newman and Mr. De Theret on Monday. Will you keep your ears open?"

"You know I can't hear anything through those walls. And besides, if it's confidential—"

"Anything," Gertie pressed. "Whatever you can find out. After all, my job could be at stake. And at my age . . ."

Rita understood. She hoped her own graying roots didn't show. "I'll try to find out as much as I can."

"Thanks."

Gertie took another bite of salad and gave herself a mental pat on the back. This undercover stuff seemed pretty easy. And not too dangerous, so far.

CHAPTER THIRTY

Business, or Pleasure?

Houston Intercontinental Airport was bursting with travelers when Kevin Molton arrived at the international ticketing area. No luggage carts were in sight. He wrestled his bags toward the nearest ticket counter and looked around for E.B. Odom.

Even from behind, she was easy to spot in the first-class line. Surrounded by leopard-print luggage, she had poured herself into a thin white velour jogging suit that revealed every nuance of her professionally sculpted body. At the tightest places, her skin glowed pink through the fabric. She bent over to zip one of her bags.

The men in line behind her jockeyed for a clear view. Molton imagined their mental calculations as he approached the line. Thong, or no thong?

Thong, he determined, as he got nearer. The thin silk of her low-cut camisole barely covered her ample cleavage and did nothing to mask her nipples. He shivered, part in fear and part excitement.

She stood up when she saw him. She was talking on her phone.

"Gotta go," she said into the phone. "I said, I have got to go. We'll discuss this when I get back. In the meantime, do your job right, for a change." She snapped the phone off and tossed it into her purse.

She shot eye daggers at Molton. "Could you be any later?"

"Sorry." He dropped his bags next to hers and wondered who she'd been talking to that made her so angry. Better not ask.

"Don't ever keep me waiting like this again," she hissed.

"Sorry." He stood silently beside her until it was their turn at the ticket counter.

E.B. extracted their tickets from her purse and handed them over.

The ticket agent asked for their passports.

Molton pulled his from his jacket pocket. E.B. handed hers to him. He stared at its cover, unable to think of what to do next.

"Passports?" the agent repeated.

Recovering, Molton handed the documents to the agent, who looked them over for what seemed like an eternity.

"Traveling together?"

Again, Molton froze.

E.B. gave him a disgusted look and took over. "Together."

"Business, or pleasure?"

E.B. smiled. "A little of both, I hope." She threaded her arm under Molton's and gave it a little squeeze.

"Bags to check?"

"Two each," E.B. replied, still smiling at the agent. "Kevin, dear, please put them on the scale for us. And here, carry this one on board for me." She handed him the smallest leopard bag.

He did as she directed. The agent tagged the bags, attached the claim stubs to their tickets and gave them to Molton. "Gate seventeen. It's on time. Have a nice trip."

E.B. hooked her arm under his again and they headed toward the gate.

"Relax," she whispered. "Try not to look like you're going to the dentist. Act like you like being with me."

"I do like being with you, E.B. It's just that I'm not used to—"

"No more talk. Relax and enjoy the trip. We'll have a drink or two on the plane and you'll be fine. Just don't spoil the party. That makes me grouchy. You don't want me to be grouchy, do you?"

"No. I—"

"Of course not. Today's the first day of the rest of your life, Kevin, the life you've always wanted."

"I know," he replied. "And I'm ready for it, E.B. I am. Ready for . . . everything. It's just happening so fast. I . . . I guess I'm still a little overwhelmed by the confidence you and Mr. De Theret . . . by the confidence that you . . . and he—"

"Stop!" She jerked him to a halt. "Enough talk about business for now. Loosen up! Enjoy yourself.

I'm up for some fun. I thought you were, too." She took off without him.

"Of course I am," he answered when he caught up. He tried to make it sound like he meant it. He still found it hard to believe this woman really wanted to be with him. Soon he'd get the chance to prove himself. With all the pressure riding on this trip, he hoped he'd be up to the task.

"This is our gate," she said. She took his arm again and squeezed it. "Here we go."

They joined the line to board, and soon they were on the plane. As he took his assigned seat next to E.B., he said a silent prayer.

CHAPTER THIRTY-ONE

Magnets

Saturday's ride to Serenity Ranch was blissfully uneventful, a welcome change from the oppressive strain of the week. Samantha was determined to keep things light with Carter Chapman. He seemed to be trying, too.

"I have a joke I think you'll like," she announced.

He glanced at her in mock surprise. "You have a joke, for me? I had the distinct impression that you hate jokes."

"This one's right up your alley. Besides, I don't hate jokes. I just think yours are . . ."

"Cute?"

"I was going to say corny."

"Ouch. I thought you said they were cute."

"Well, I'll tell you this joke, and you can make fun of me, too. Deal?"

"Deal."

"Okay, here goes. Ready?"

He nodded.

"How do you tell a girl chromosome from a boy chromosome?"

He thought for a moment, then shook his head. "I have no idea. How *do* you tell a girl chromosome from a boy chromosome?"

She gave him a big smile. "You pull down their genes!"

A slow grin spread across his face. "Did you just tell me a dirty joke?"

"No! It's cute."

"How is it that all my jokes are corny, and this one is cute?"

"Some people have a knack."

"Okay, now you asked for it. I saved some of my best material for the ride up today. Prepare to be amused."

"Amused or abused?"

"You decide. When we get to my place, if you don't like the jokes, dinner's on me. If they make you laugh, dinner's still on me. Deal?"

"Deal."

He grinned in triumph. "I'm a winner either way."

She smiled back. Yes, definitely a winner.

The farther they drove from the city, the more her spirits lifted. Chapman seemed cheerier too. Maybe it was all for show, this unspoken truce between them. Or maybe it would last.

Samantha stopped in the front entry hall of Chapman's grand house to take in the airy expanse. Afternoon sunlight poured in through the beveled glass panels that flanked the front door and spread tiny rainbow dots on every surface. A chandelier, festooned with antlers and cut crystals, hung low above a round oak table that occupied the center of the space.

"I'd forgotten how grand this place is."

Chapman took her bag. "You were a little preoccupied last time."

Preoccupied was one word for it. Between worry over Lista and fear that Chapman believed that she was some kind of felon, she'd been barely conscious of anything else.

At her feet, heavy-grained wood flooring spread toward the adjoining rooms. It covered the steps of the grand staircase, too, as it curved upward along the wall. "What kind of wood is this?"

"Mesquite. Grows in abundance around here. Hard as a brick. Mostly, it's used to grill Texas barbecue."

"I know what mesquite tastes like. But I've never seen it used like this. It's great-looking, especially for a country place."

Carter took her bag and set it by the bottom step of the stairway. "Why don't you relax while I get a few things together for dinner? Since we kind of missed lunch, I figured we'd have an early supper."

"Sounds good." She followed him into the kitchen. "Where is your . . . Dottie?"

"I gave her the weekend off so she could take her grandkids to San Antonio."

"And your caretaker, or chauffeur, or whatever he is?"

"Ralph? He's doing work for me in the city today."

"So, it's just the two of us?" The possibilities played in her brain.

"Hope you don't mind." He opened the refrigerator and set some food on the counter. "I'll grill these steaks, bake a couple of potatoes and make a salad. It's not the five-course dinner Dottie usually produces, but it's kind of my go-to menu on weekends. And if I know Dottie, she left a few goodies for later."

"Sounds great. Can I help?"

"Relax and enjoy. As a matter of fact, it's so beautiful outside, why don't you do some exploring before it gets dark? When you get back, you can help me watch the steaks on the grill."

She gave him a mischievous wink. "Okay. I'll come back for the grilling, though I hoped we'd gotten past all that."

Samantha had intended to do as Chapman suggested and go outside, but when she returned to the grand entry, curiosity drew her toward the curved stairway.

Along the wall as it wound upward hung a series of old framed maps. She hadn't paid much attention to them the first time she saw them. Now, she lingered at the one at the bottom.

Drawn by a 16th-century cartographer, the map showed a vague shape of North America. Much of the south and west of the landmass was identified as *Nueva Espana*, New Spain, the territory recently claimed by the Spanish crown. Though there seemed to have been a lot of guessing at the geography, the positioning of the Gulf of Mexico looked familiar.

A few steps up, the next map delineated Texas as a possession of France. The next, showed the territory as part of greater Mexico. Near the second-floor landing hung a map representing the Republic of Texas, the independent nation.

Samantha reached the second floor and hesitated. The bathroom she'd used to freshen up on her first visit was just ahead. Curiosity got the best of her. She kept going and opened the next door.

It was a child's bedroom. White eyelet curtains festooned the windows and the four-poster bed. Raggedy Ann and Raggedy Andy dolls rested on the pillows. She walked in.

A few framed photographs sat atop a white-painted chest of drawers. She picked one up and studied it. Two children, a boy and girl, both about five or six, posed for the camera in a field of bluebonnets. She reached for another photo: the same children, a little older, with a blond woman standing behind them. The three of them were smiling and squinting in the sun. Chapman's family. All of them gone.

She stared at the photos for a long time, peering into the faces, imagining what each must have been like in life. Her eyes brimmed with tears. It was impossible to fathom the loss. She set the pictures down and left the room, closing the door behind her.

In the hallway, she hesitated. The next room most likely held the boy's bed, and further down the hall, Chapman's bedroom. She'd already invaded one private, sorrowful space without his permission. She decided not to go on.

Returning to the staircase, she continued upward.

The third-floor landing was much smaller, with only three doors. The first one revealed a large old-fashioned black and white tiled bathroom with porcelain fixtures and a claw-footed tub. Nice.

The second door opened to a closet full of office supplies. At the third door, a security keypad barred entrance.

Hmmm. Why would Chapman need this kind of security in a country house?

A voice boomed from somewhere in the hallway, startling her. "Ready for the grilling?" It was Chapman.

Mortified that she'd been caught snooping, she turned in all directions to look for him, but no one was there. "Where are you?"

"Look up, behind you," said the voice.

She turned around. A camera attached to the ceiling occupied a corner of the hallway. Next to it was a small speaker.

Oh.

He was the one to apologize. "Sorry for the Big Brother stuff. When you're a government contractor, it's best to know who goes in and out of here. Don't worry, I know you're not a spy."

"Even though you caught me sneaking around?"

"You're welcome to snoop. I have no secrets. Not from you, anyway. But before you learn every boring thing there is to know about me, let's eat."

Supper on the veranda was almost over when the sun began its evening swoon toward the horizon.

Samantha savored the last morsel. For the first time in weeks, she was enjoying herself. "That steak was delicious!"

Chapman beamed at the compliment. "I told you, it's my specialty. Glad you liked it."

"Did you use mesquite to flavor it?"

"Sorry, but the chef never reveals his secrets."

"I thought you said you had no secrets."

"I lied," he said playfully. "Some things I'll never tell, especially when they concern my recipe for grilled T-bone. That's top secret. Besides, you probably learned enough about me when you were upstairs."

She winced. "I didn't mean to pry. The maps along the staircase caught my eye, and then I found myself on the second floor and I just—"

"Got curious?" He seemed to be enjoying her discomfort.

"Well, yes," she admitted. "You said 'explore away,' so I did. I'm sorry if I overstepped."

"Not at all. I meant what I said. I want you to be comfortable here." His eyes caught hers and held them.

She was embarrassed and grateful at the same time. It was baffling, how he could make her feel so many emotions mixed up together. She lowered her eyes, not knowing what to say.

He was the one to break the silence. "So, what did you see on your little tour?"

She took a gulp of wine and realized she was getting a little tipsy. "You have a very nice house."

"And?"

"Very neat housekeeping."

He smiled. "And?"

She searched for something neutral to mention. Anything but the photos. No need to bring up unhappy memories tonight.

"The maps," she said at last. "Fascinating."

"They're historic treasures. Came with the house."

"Really interesting." She hoped he wouldn't press her on the rest of her prowlings.

"How did you like the third floor?"

"The third floor?" She took another gulp of wine. "Well, as you know, there wasn't much to see. Impressive security for a country place."

"That's where I keep my secret steak recipe." He grinned. "Unfortunately, it's off limits."

His face turned serious. "It's where I work most of the time. Maybe someday I can show it to you. Anyway, it's about the least interesting space in the house. Just an office, really."

He seemed happy to end the conversation there. She relaxed again.

"I'm glad you invited me today, Carter." Feeling his name on her lips for the first time was like taking the first sip of brandy. A tiny shock, and then a warm glow.

"Let's clear the table," he said. "Then we can come back and finish the wine."

By the time they returned to the veranda, the sun had dropped behind a stand of ancient oak trees. Crimson rays glowed beyond the branches. Evening birdsong and the chirrup of frogs rose in a twilight serenade. They stood together at the railing, taking it in.

"This place is beautiful at sunset," she said. "I can see why it's called Serenity. There's no better word for it."

"It certainly was once." He put his arm around her. "It's beginning to feel like it again."

She turned away from the last of the sun and looked up at him. Without hesitating, he leaned down to kiss her. The moment she felt his lips on hers, she melted.

He pulled her closer to him. His arms encircled her, and he kissed her again and again, hungry for more.

"I don't want to take you home, Samantha," he whispered. "Not tonight."

"I don't want to go." She met his kisses with her own pent-up longing.

On Monday, ugly reality would intrude again. She pushed thoughts of her meeting with De Theret into the recesses of her consciousness and let herself relax.

Tonight, the magnets were aligned, and there was no holding back.

Falling into Place

Samantha was nearly breathless as she entered the back door to the kitchen where Carter was busy making breakfast. The morning breeze had tossed her hair in all directions, but she didn't care. The scent of coffee and waffles greeted her.

"Smells yummy in here!" She stuck a bunch of bluebonnets and Indian paintbrush into a tall glass, filled it with water and set it on the table. "Flowers for the chef."

"Have fun?" He lifted a fresh waffle from the griddle and added it to a growing pile on the platter.

"It was glorious! All the colors and smells of new green, and the wind whipping everything around! Everything shimmering in the sun. This place is so beautiful. Perfect."

"And your perfect breakfast is about to begin." He carried the plate of waffles and a pitcher of syrup to the kitchen table. "Sit. Dig in."

"Such service!"

"You ain't see nuthin' yet, ma'am." He set a platter of scrambled eggs and a bowl of fresh berries on the table, sat beside her and began piling eggs on her plate.

She grabbed his wrist to keep him from adding another heaping spoonful. "No more, please! What do you think I am, the U.S. Army?"

"The way I saw you put away egg rolls, I'd say you're more like the Chinese army. Besides, these are incredibly delicious. If I took some away, you'd just want more." He set the overburdened plate in front of her.

She made a face to protest, but truth was, the eggs smelled great. "Pass the syrup, please." She doused her plate with the sweet liquid and took a bite of waffle. "Yum."

He freshened their coffee. "Whither did you wander on your walk this morning?"

"All over, really. I found an ancient barn with an antique tractor in it. And the stables. Beautiful horses. The palomino and I made friends, I think. And an old well. It was covered in brambles with white flowers just beginning to bloom on them. Maybe blackberry?"

"Around here, folks call them dewberries. Dottie makes the best jam you ever tasted from those things."

"So did my Mom," Samantha said. The sudden memory jolted her.

"I'll bet she did." He reached out and clasped her hand. "Sounds like you made a full sweep of the back forty."

She had left out one sight she had come across, one that she hesitated to mention. There were so many unanswered questions about the man sitting across from her. But if their relationship continued, she needed to understand what had sparked its beginning.

"I came back to the house down a path that brought me past the little cemetery again."

A momentary flicker of pain crossed his face.

"I'm sorry," she said softly. "I wasn't going to mention it. I wanted us to have a good time today."

He stared into his coffee mug.

"Is it okay if we talk about your family?" She took his silence for permission to continue.

"I stood there for a long time, looking at their graves. At first, it seemed like we have so much in common, you and I. Losing our families, I mean. But that's not entirely true. What I lost was my past, and the people who could remember it with me. But you lost your future, your hopes and dreams for your children, the pleasure of watching them grow, the love of your wife, the joy of building a life together."

He sat, rigid, as she catalogued his pain.

"For me, there are things I'll never know. No one is left to fill in details about my childhood, answer questions about my family history. I was angry about that for a long time. Still am, really. Angry, and sad. But to have your future cut off like that. How do you deal with the bitterness?"

"Bitterness?" He chewed on the word as if it were a nasty seed.

"You couldn't have been satisfied when that drunk driver got off without punishment."

His back stiffened. "I wasn't."

"How did you handle it?"

He did not answer.

She'd already broached the subject. Might as well forge ahead. "You are so focused on bringing the people at De Theret to justice for me, and I'm grateful for that. But what about the person who killed your—"

"Stop!" He bolted to the door, then wheeled around, a strange fury in his eyes. "This is not the time."

"Please. I want to know."

"Why—today of all days—do you want to bring up every damn thing that's painful to me? I'm working hard to get past it, to be with you, to have one minute of happiness."

"But I—"

He yanked the back door open and stormed out.

She rose to go after him, but she didn't get far.

He stormed back in as fast as he'd exited and slammed the door shut behind him. "You want to know? Okay. Here it is."

His voice rumbled through clenched teeth. "It was Vinson De Theret! He went by a different name back then, but he's the one. That no good, lousy drunk destroyed my family and kept on going. Living his life like nothing, like nothing . . ."

He spun around and was out the door again.

De Theret! How could she have missed it?

Everything snapped into focus. Carter Chapman had been nearing the end of his epic, meticulously charted course of retribution when she came into the mix and complicated his plan.

She finally understood why he was so determined to protect her, like he hadn't been able to do for his wife and children. She rushed out the door to follow him.

She found him at the porch railing, staring out beyond the willows. When she approached, he turned and met her halfway. He reached out and pulled her to him, holding her so close it was hard to know where she ended and he began.

"I'm sorry," she whispered. "I'm so, so sorry."

More than ever, she was committed to her plan. But they had one more day together, one last chance to push the fear and sadness away, before the world started spinning again.

She buried herself deep within his arms and held tight.

Monday morning came much too soon. Samantha and Carter had stayed at Serenity overnight, pushing back against the inevitable. Soon after the sunlight reanimated the gentle folds of earth surrounding the house, they headed back to the city.

They stood in her living room and clung to each other.

"I may not see you for a couple of days," he said. "Promise me you won't do anything foolish."

She let her body melt into his, but she did not answer him.

He stood back and held her by the shoulders, searching her face. "Sam?"

She let the subject hang between them. "What will you be doing?"

"With a little luck, we'll be able to wrap up E.B. Odom. It will take some intricate inter-agency coordination, but we're hoping to pull it off. Timing is crucial. It either comes together now, or it's twiddle-our-thumbs time until the next opportunity presents itself."

She pulled away. "E.B.? But you're after Vinson De Theret."

"At this point, I'll take what I can get. We're still not sure which one of them is responsible for the car bomb, or for Lista's death."

"But you want De Theret," she argued. "Can't you get him, too?"

"Odom is a pretty sure bet. The hope is that, once she's caught, she'll implicate him. It's the best chance we have, so we're going for it."

"Sounds like you're counting on a lot of pieces to fall into place."

"If everything works out, she'll be in custody by tonight. And if she gives us the critical information we need about De Theret's illicit operations, we'll get him too."

"Seems a little iffy."

"It's not as clean as I'd like," he admitted. "But based on what we know of Odom's character, it shouldn't take much to get her to roll on him."

Samantha sensed that something was being sacrificed on her behalf. "I can take care of myself better than you think. Please don't jeopardize this on my account."

He held her close again. "I'm trying to do what's best for both of us. Just promise me you'll be careful. I need to know that you're safe."

She avoided his gaze. "I'll be fine."

"Look at me and say that."

Her eyes met his. "I'll be fine. You'd better go if you want to save the world by tonight, Superman."

He checked his watch. "You're right." He kissed her on the forehead, and with a backward look, was gone.

She stood in the middle of her living room and tried to conjure the afterglow of their weekend together, the last peaceful moments before their separate missions were completed. But the spell was broken.

While everyone else pursued E.B. Odom, the necessity of bringing Vinson De Theret to justice could not be left to chance. She would give Carter the inside help he'd sought from the beginning, even if he no longer wanted it.

Everything depended her. Carter's peace of mind, and even her ultimate survival.

Only an hour to go until she met with Vinson. Time to get ready.

CHAPTER THIRTY-THREE

Money on the Side

Vinson De Theret greeted her at his office door. "Good to see you looking so well, Samantha."

The warm greeting did not hide his discomfort. His pale, red-rimmed eyes scanned her expression for clues to why she had asked to see him. An array of spasms played across his face. He did not like surprises.

Her pulse ran a hundred-yard dash as she crossed the mauve carpet and dropped into a low-slung leather chair in front of his desk.

De Theret sat behind the desk, eyes guarded. "No calls, Rita," he ordered through the intercom. He cleared his throat and looked at Samantha expectantly. "What can I do for you?"

She struggled to keep her composure. Lying was not her preferred mode of operation, but in order for her plan to work, she had to muster as much hutzpah as she could.

De Theret was waiting for her to say something. She could only hope the right words would come to her.

"I . . . I don't know how to begin."

"Why don't we start with how you are feeling?"

"Oh, I . . . I feel fine." This tongue-tied turmoil would never do. She pushed through. "I'm okay, really. One hundred per cent."

"Ready to come back to work?"

She hesitated. It was now, or never. She cleared her throat. "Yes . . . and no."

"Yes and no? What's that mean?" He leaned back and crossed his arms, regarding her from under his white-tipped eyelashes.

She watched the red rims of his milky-blue eyes as they opened and closed and opened again in anticipation.

Here goes.

"I mean, I'm ready to work. I'm healthy. I feel good. But I'm not sure I want my job back."

His blinking stopped. "Really?"

"I am grateful for the opportunity you've given me, Vinson. And looking back, I think I've been an important part of the growth of this company and contributed my fair share."

"More than that."

"Thanks. But there's not really much more for me to accomplish here. And, the truth is, I'm tired of . . . of . . ."

She hoped he couldn't see her right leg jerking involuntarily. She crossed her legs the other way, exposing more thigh than she'd intended.

His eyes followed the movement and rested there. "Tired of . . . ?"

"Oh, I don't know," she said. "It's just that, since Derek um, died, and Lista left . . . I've been thinking."

De Theret tore his gaze from her legs to search her expression. His eyes were wary again. "Thinking? Thinking about what?"

His voice held a defensive edge. Had he taken the mention of Derek and Lista as some kind of threat? Not good. The conversation was getting trickier to navigate.

Back off, choose your words. "Oh, just contemplating life in general, I guess, and what it all means."

The Little Girl Lost approach seemed to put him at ease. Showing more thigh had probably helped too. She felt a little more confident.

"It's just that, Derek meant more to me than anyone ever knew. Long before I came here, he had rescued me from the depths of a life filled with . . . well, shall we say . . . insouciance."

By his look, she wasn't sure he understood the word. Maybe she was being too subtle.

She tried again. "You may not be aware that my family was killed while I was at college."

His eyes widened, then narrowed. He started blinking again. Was this part of her story a problem, too?

She recovered quickly. "A house fire. Nobody's fault."

He seemed to relax a bit.

The next part was critical. Everything hinged on her ability to tell what could sound like an incredible tale.

She took a deep breath. "When my family died, I was lost. And broke. I fell in with a group of girls at college who made lots of money—on the side, so to speak. I was hurting so much that a life full of . . . of impersonal relationships, seemed easier to deal with. Plus, I could make a lot of money. And I did." She stopped to let the story sink in.

He leaned forward. "You did . . . what, exactly?"

It felt like he was starting to follow her meaning.

"Well, I didn't exactly sell Girl Scout cookies."

Silence hung in the air like an executioner's blade.

He swiveled from side to side in his chair. "Why are you telling me this?"

You're in it now, Samantha. Bring it home. "Well, some of us got into a little trouble, back then. Derek Grey was my lawyer. He pulled me out of that life and made sure I stayed in school, like my parents would have wanted. It's because of him that I am who I am today."

Tears pooled in the corners of her eyes. De Theret offered a tissue. She blotted and waited for him to process what she had told him.

There was a grain of truth in the story, and that tiny kernel had helped her eyes overflow. She felt a twinge of guilt, using Derek to fabricate a lie, but if her genuine tears for him had helped her make this counterfeit version of their history seem true, so be it. Only the future mattered now.

She took stock of her performance so far. It seemed to be working. But the crucial test lay ahead. She had to convince De Theret that the story was completely true.

She re-crossed her legs the other way and blotted her eyes again. "I don't even know why I'm telling you this, except that . . . I don't have anyone else." More tears welled up. This time, they were mostly of the crocodile variety.

She broke off, blotted her eyes and turned her gaze to the window, struggling to stay in the moment. The wait seemed interminable until De Theret spoke.

"I've always had a soft spot for you, Samantha. From the moment I first interviewed you."

She held her breath, hoping he'd continue.

He stopped swiveling. "How can I help?"

Almost there. She stifled a smile behind the moist tissue. "Help? Oh, I didn't come here to ask you for anything, Vinson. I just thought I owed it to you to explain in person why I'm quitting."

"I'd like to help you. It would mean a great deal to me."

"Well, I don't think I'll need a letter of reference." She offered a wry smile.

The rest of her speech tumbled out exactly like she'd rehearsed it. "I've already talked to the man I used to work for. He said he'd take me back, if I'd relocate. So, I'll probably be moving away soon."

She wasn't sure how to continue, or if she should. Best not to pressure him. Just be quiet and let everything sink in.

"Let me help you. There may be something I can do that you're not aware of."

Her pulse quickened. "Oh, Vinson, you've done so much for me already."

"I want to do this. Give me the guy's name, the one you used to work for. I'll see what we can work out."

"I don't understand." Her heart was turning somersaults.

"Never mind that now. Just let me see what I can do. What did you say his name was?"

"Angelo. Angelo Infante. Some people call him The Angel."

De Theret's eyes lit up. "Angelo Infante? You have his number?"

She nodded. "The service I worked for was one of his." She tried to keep her hands from shaking while she searched for the number. "Here it is. Angel's Coeds. He won't talk to you personally unless you use my name."

"Okay. I'll talk to the guy. Maybe we can work something out. I hate to see valuable talent like yours get away, Samantha. It would be a terrible, terrible waste."

"I still don't understand . . ."

He would not commit himself any further. "I'm a businessman. So is he. Just give me time to talk to him. And don't make any rash decisions until you hear from me."

He rose and strode to the door. "I'm glad you opened up to me. I know you will be, too."

She stared across the desk at his empty chair. What had just happened? She guessed her plan was working. But now that this part was over, it almost seemed too easy. De Theret had taken the bait, hadn't he?

There was nothing to do but leave the man to his own twisted thoughts and wait for the result.

She collected herself and joined him at the door.

"Thank you for understanding, Vinson," she mumbled. "Sorry I unloaded on you like that."

"Not to worry," he assured her. "These things always work out for the best."

CHAPTER THIRTY-FOUR

Jaws

To exterminate the slimy feeling she had worn home from her meeting with Vinson De Theret, Samantha stripped off her clothes first thing and turned on the shower.

Under the hot stream of water, the calming scent of freesia shampoo helped a little. But nothing could stop the replay of their conversation from looping endlessly in her brain.

De Theret had bought her story. And Angelo had promised to do his part when he got the call. So far, so good.

As she toweled dry, the doorbell rang. She wasn't expecting anyone. It could be Carter on a lunch break. Maybe he had come with good news. She slipped on her robe and flew downstairs.

A peek through the keyhole revealed a pimply-faced boy with a cap that read Third Coast Florist. She opened the door. Under his arm he held a long white cardboard box tied with a wide green ribbon.

"Samantha Newman? Express delivery for you." He shoved the box toward her and returned to his van.

Samantha took the box and fairly floated into the kitchen. Carter hadn't come, but he'd sent flowers. Who else would be so thoughtful? Eagerly, she peeled away the layers of green tissue paper to uncover two dozen long-stemmed red roses. Beautiful.

She lifted the card that nestled among the blossoms and read it.

"To happy endings and new beginnings." It was signed: "Vinson."

She recoiled from the box as if it held a nest of spiders. Incredulous, she read the card again. Dread rose in her throat.

The telephone rang. She checked the caller ID. This time, it was Carter Chapman.

"I took a break for a minute to say I'm thinking about you." The sound of his voice halted her momentary panic.

"Thanks. I could use some positive reinforcement at the moment."

"What's wrong?"

"Oh, I'm okay. Just trying to hang in there."

It was much too early to let him in on her plan. He'd just try to talk her out of it. Later, when everything was set, she'd need his cooperation. And by then it would be too late for him to argue.

"I called earlier, but you didn't answer." He waited for an explanation, but she gave none.

He persisted. "Did you go out?"

"Yes, for a little while."

"Where did you go?"

"To the office." Telling him the truth was probably a mistake. Why hadn't she said she ran to the drugstore?

"You went back to . . . to . . . But you said you wouldn't. You promised." Astonishment and disappointment colored his words.

"I didn't go back to work."

"Then what were you doing there?"

"I had a meeting with De Theret."

"Vinson De Theret? What the—"

"Just to talk about things."

"Things?"

"My job. I told him I was thinking about resigning."

"Thinking about it? You told him that?" Carter sounded like he was ready to jump through the phone.

"Yes."

"What did he say?"

She was running out of evasions, and Carter was getting more and more worked up. Time to end the conversation.

"It's kind of a long story. And you have a lot to do, so—"

"What did he say, Sam?"

"We sort of left things up in the air."

"I can't believe you actually went—*what?*" Someone in the background spoke to him. "Sam, I have to go. Let's finish this tonight. I don't know when I'll get free, but if it's late, I can let myself in with the key you gave me."

If they were face to face before she was ready to share her plan, it would be too hard to keep it from him. She needed time to let the conversation between

De Theret and Angelo Infante play out first. When the time was right, she would definitely need Carter's help. But not before everything else was in place.

"Don't worry about me, Carter. I'm fine being alone tonight. I'm kinda beat, anyway."

There was silence on the other end of the phone.

"Carter?"

"Please don't make me worry about you like this, Sam."

"I'll be fine. Honest. I'll be very careful. I don't plan to go back to the office tomorrow, if that's what you're worried about. Do what you have to do. I'll be safe. I promise."

"Okay. I might get stuck here in an all-nighter, anyway. See you tomorrow. Take care." He hung up.

Samantha took a deep breath and returned to the problem of the roses, still resting in their long white box. She liked having fresh flowers in the house, and these were particularly pretty. But the sight of them made her stomach churn.

She tore the card into tiny pieces, dropped them on top of the flowers, and closed the box. Hefting the box and its contents off the counter with one hand, she opened the trash compactor with the other. With a firm shove, she forced the box as deep into the bin as it would go and crumpled the sides and corners until it all fit inside.

She slammed the compactor shut and pushed the start button. Grinding and groaning sounds signaled that the bin's contents were suffering a cruel demise. A terrible fate for such lovely, innocent flowers.

Too bad she couldn't have saved the roses and pushed Vinson De Theret into the garbage instead. But his gesture of friendship was not entirely wasted. As the masher's jaws did their work, Samantha began to feel better.

CHAPTER THIRTY-FIVE

Smarty Britches

Weary as she felt from the day's ups and downs, Samantha lay awake all night with every painful chapter of her life replaying in her head.

Breaking up with Derek, the car explosion, Derek's death, Lista's letter, the desolation after the fire that killed her family, her meeting with Vinson De Theret and the dangerous path it put her on: all of it spooled into a waking nightmare. She tried to conjure more pleasant images, but she was helpless against the onslaught.

Dawn broke, full of wind and thunder. Newly budded branches of a pecan tree scraped ominously against the bedroom window. *My life story, complete with Shakespearean sound effects.*

The blustery weather made a fitting backdrop for the morning. After the meeting with De Theret yesterday, there was nothing to do but wait for the game to play out. Might as well take it easy while she could.

She turned off the alarm, fluffed her pillow, and snuggled under the covers again.

After what seemed like only minutes, the telephone rang. She rolled over and checked the time. Almost noon. She sat up, cleared her throat, and reached for the phone.

"Hello?" She hoped she sounded reasonably alert.

"Samantha?"

Her heart sank.

"Yes, Vinson."

"Did I wake you?"

"No."

"I just wanted to tell you that I talked to your friend Angelo."

"You did?" If she hadn't been fully awake before, she was now. She sat up, her heart racing. "What did he say?"

"He said you were the best he ever had."

She winced. "He did?"

What was she supposed to say now? She squeezed her eyes shut to defog her brain, but nothing came. Maybe if she waited long enough, De Theret would say something.

He did. "I have a client for you."

"Client?"

"One of our best. I think you'll really like him. All the girls do."

She cleared her throat to tamp down the rising bile. "Who?"

"Someone I think you'll like. Someone I trust to treat you with the respect you deserve."

Her heart was going a mile a minute. She bolted out of bed and began to pace. "But, I . . . uh. . . I'm not sure I . . . I'm not sure I'm . . . ready."

"But this is the job you said you wanted." He sounded perturbed. "I told you I would handle things.

You don't even have to relocate. Angelo was sorry to hear you wouldn't be working for him, but I told him I'd take good care of you."

"But how did you work it out so fast?"

"You know me. When I put my mind to something, it doesn't take long to make things happen. Especially when it's for people I care about."

Something nasty rose in her throat again. "But we, uh, we haven't exactly made a deal yet, Vinson. Couldn't we wait until—"

"What for? You needed help, and I came through for you. Besides, the appointment is this evening. Too late to cancel now."

"Today?"

"Six o'clock."

She was stunned into silence. She'd worked out the whole idea in her head, but she hadn't planned for things to move this fast.

"It will be well worth your time, Samantha. I promise. Most of our girls take home two thousand a night, minimum."

Our girls! He said *our girls!* Why hadn't she thought to get her voice recorder ready for his call?

De Theret kept talking. "But if you're as good as Angelo says you are, you could make much more."

"More?" She had to slow things down, stall until her brain could catch up. "Vinson, what do you mean 'our girls'? Are you . . . are you saying . . .?"

"Come on, Samantha. This is no time to play coy. You know exactly what I'm talking about. We'll discuss details later. This appointment has to happen today. Trust me."

She could tell he was beginning to lose patience. Better to continue the charade, at least for now, until she could think of what to do next.

"What's the client's name?"

"Just ask for Mr. Doyle's room at Hotel ZaZa. He'll be waiting for you there. I'm trusting you, Samantha. Don't let me down." He hung up.

She stood, immobile, at the foot of her bed and gaped at the phone, wondering what to do.

Yesterday, she had hoped that the meeting with De Theret would open the door to the secret operations that Carter had told her about. Though her performance in his office was an apparent success, she wasn't as prepared for the next step as she thought she would be.

Okay, Miss Smarty Britches, now what? Her terror-stricken reflection in the mirror stared back at her. Now what, indeed.

It was time to get Carter involved. He would be angry that she had kept her plan from him. And furious that she had even contemplated such a strategy. But she was committed now. He would understand that, and he'd see to it that she was protected.

She dialed his number. Voicemail. She left a message for him to call her as soon as he picked it up. Then she hung up and dialed the FBI number he'd given her as backup.

"Carter Chapman?" The agent who answered sounded puzzled.

"Yes, Carter Chapman. I need to speak to him. It's urgent."

"What division does he work for?"

"Division? I don't know. He told me to use this number if I needed to reach him. And I do. It's an emergency."

"The name's familiar, but I don't think he works here," the man said. "Is he an agent?"

"A consultant."

"Who's he working with?"

Her heart sank. "I don't know. He never gave me anyone's name."

"Sorry, I'm just answering the phone here," the man told her. "Everyone in this section is in the field today. If he works with them, he's probably out with them now."

"All day?"

"Yes ma'am, I think so. Can someone else help you?"

Samantha momentarily considered the question. "It would take too much time to explain. I need Mr. Chapman. Is there any other way to reach him?"

"Not that I know of."

"I can keep trying to call his mobile, I guess."

"I suppose. Except, he may be off the grid until he calls in."

"It's extremely urgent. If I leave a message with you, could you try to get it to him, or at least make sure he gets it immediately? Tell him to call Samantha. It's urgent."

She hung up and dialed Chapman's cell phone again. No answer. She still had a few hours to reach him.

No reason to panic. So why was she trembling?

CHAPTER THIRTY-SIX

Toppers

Chapman cursed the storm that was delaying dozens of flights at Houston Intercontinental Airport, including the one he was primed to meet. He checked his watch.

By the time the control tower had cleared the schedule, thousands of flight-weary souls would pour into the baggage claim area, pushing and shoving and jockeying for positions at the luggage conveyor belts. And the greater the commotion, the more chances there would be for complications.

Once the storm had passed, Chapman's vision became reality. Arriving international passengers streamed in, filling the vast space with a bazaar of languages, aromas, and fashions. The demand for luggage carts outstripped the supply, forcing the unlucky to drag, push, kick or otherwise tease their heavy loads toward the lengthening U.S. Customs inspection lines.

His eyes searched across the bedraggled throng to locate Mack Maginnis. The agent and several other men and women in crisp business suits were carefully studying the crowd from the other side, each of them ready for the big show, when the flight they awaited would arrive.

In contrast to the raucous hubbub, a calm, modulated voice spoke over the public address system. "Announcing the arrival of Aviateca Airlines flight three-sixteen. Passengers will deplane at gate forty-two and proceed directly to U.S. customs." That was the one.

Maginnis gave the signal. Slowly, the agents shifted closer to the Customs area. All was ready.

As Chapman turned to join them, a sharp pain pierced the back of his thigh.

Half stumbling, he spun around to find himself confronted by the backside of a large woman. She was bent over, struggling to retrieve the scatterings of an overturned knitting basket. Her hand clutched the culprit needle.

He ignored the pain and knelt to help her gather the half-dozen or so balls of yarn that had rolled toward the feet of other distracted travelers.

"Devil take this blasted basket!" the red-faced woman muttered in a British accent. She wheezed heavily from her efforts. "I had a hellish time fitting it into my checked bag, and when I yanked it free, the entire thing turned toppers on me."

She smoothed loose strands of gray hair away from her flushed face and held the wicker hamper open for Chapman to toss the last ball of wool inside.

"So kind," she said. "Sorry for the trouble."

"No problem." He pushed the knitting needles deeper into the basket. "Just be careful where you stick those."

"Oh, they are quite harmless," she laughed, unaware of the pain they had inflicted. He rubbed the back of his leg and turned away.

The distraction had allowed crucial minutes to elapse. He had to regain his bearings. He moved nearer to the Customs area and searched the crowd for Maginnis's team. All were accounted for, though none had spotted the couple they sought.

The pair were sure to be among the jostling crowd by now. His eyes scanned the lines, briefly lingering on each face.

There they were, toward the back of the line, looking like ordinary business travelers. At least, the man did, in his gray suit and tortoise-rimmed glasses. The woman, on the other hand, looked far from ordinary, though she was dressed in a business suit.

Her navy pinstriped skirt stopped high above her delicate knees, with a long slit up to her thigh. The matching jacket that hugged her waist was burst open at breast level to accommodate her large bosom. A leopard-print attaché hung by a thin leather strap from her shoulder.

While she waited in line, the woman consulted a compact mirror and finger-combed her tousled coiffure. Even without a photo to work from, it was easy to pick E.B. Odom from the crowd.

Maginnis made a slight motion to the others. Two moved in from their posts to join the queue a few travelers back from the couple, while two others positioned themselves on either side of the end of the line near the agents who were randomly checking bags. Two more stood in front of the exit doors.

Chapman watched as the line inched forward. At Maginnis's signal, the customs agents moved each traveler ahead with barely a cursory glance at their bags until the line ahead of the couple in question dwindled to nothing.

Just as the pair was about to breeze through, Chapman caught the woman by the arm. "Customs check, ma'am. Come with me, please."

E.B. Odom tried to extract her arm from his grasp. "What do you think you're doing?"

He tightened his grip. "Come with me and I'll explain."

An agent took her companion's arm and led him away. Another took charge of their bags. Maginnis peeled off to join Chapman.

With two men escorting her, E.B. had no choice but to comply. She gazed up at Chapman and smiled.

"Of course, I'll come with you," she purred. "I'd be happy to. For a minute, I thought you were a mugger. You just scared me, is all. You're really very strong, you know." Her eyes glittered.

Chapman loosened his grip only slightly. He and Maginnis steered her to the examination room reserved especially for this meeting. Maginnis called in a female agent and left to phone headquarters, closing the door after him.

E.B. leaned against a wall as she worked through her options. Somebody had tipped the customs guys, though she couldn't imagine who.

She had to get herself out of there unscathed. If her bags were searched, they would find the white powder inside the expensive-looking cosmetic jars that were disguised as gifts for her many fictitious friends.

Neither of her captors spoke. She figured they must be waiting for the chubby guy to return.

She used the time to size up the two people in the room with her. The female agent, blank-faced and cheap-suited, held no interest for her. But the man? He looked slightly familiar. A face and build like that would be hard to forget, and yet, she couldn't put a place or a name to him. If she was going to get anywhere, she needed to know who he was.

He offered her a seat. She declined.

She arched her back against the wall while she studied him. Nothing jogged her memory.

Finally, curiosity go the best of her. "I hope you don't think I'm being forward, but I have to ask. Haven't we met before?"

Carter Chapman was stone-faced. "No."

She took a step toward him, hands on hips, chest at maximum exposure. "I never forget a handsome face," she purred, "and you look very familiar."

That got a smile out of him. At least he wasn't made of granite. But the smile disappeared. "We have never met before today." He shuttered again.

She was certain she had encountered him, somewhere. If he had been a regular business client at De Theret International, he might have said so. Maybe he was a customer of one of her Elite Professional girls. That was the kind of information she needed.

"Perhaps you're a client?"

A tiny reaction flickered in his eyes. "What kind of client would I be?"

"Oh, you know, a client of my business."

"What business is that?"

"Body business."

He looked slightly startled.

She was getting close to an answer, she could feel it. She crossed the room and stood close to him. "You know, bodies for hire, like office professionals, or executives. Or maybe you've used one of our more personalized services. You look like a satisfied customer."

He colored slightly. She knew she'd hit a nerve, yet she couldn't say more without incriminating herself.

She ran her fingers along the lapel of his jacket and locked her eyes on his. "I know we've met before. Don't be ashamed. It'll be our little secret." Her breasts grazed his chest. "I promise not to tell."

The female agent crossed the room and separated her from Chapman.

He straightened his jacket. "You're mistaken. We've never met."

E.B. leaned against the wall again, her eyes still riveted on him. "Pity. I think I'd enjoy doing business with you. Maybe it will come to me later, where I know you from. Everything usually does come to me. sooner or later."

A few awkward minutes passed in silence until Maginnis entered with a luggage cart that was loaded with leopard-print bags.

Chapman shot him an exasperated glance. "What the devil took so long, man?"

"Sorry." Maginnis cleared his throat and assumed an official demeanor. "Ms. Odom, I'm Gus Maginnis. My colleague here is Della Rhodes. We're federal agents." He flashed his badge. "And this is Carter Chapman."

Carter Chapman. E.B. ran the name through her memory bank. Nothing clicked.

Maginnis continued. "We have reason to believe that you are transporting illegal drugs into the United States, which is a federal offense. Take a seat, please."

She perched on a corner of the table and crossed her legs, exposing a slim thigh. "I have nothing to hide."

Maginnis read E.B. her rights. "Ms. Odom, would you please identify these cases for us?"

She kept her gaze on Chapman and did not answer.

Maginnis pressed on. "Our dogs have positively identified these bags as containing contraband drugs. The luggage tags match the stubs attached to the flight coupon with your name on it. The more cooperative you are, the easier it will go for you. Now, would you please identify the cases?"

E.B. was still focused on Chapman. She didn't recognize his name. But the face . . . If she could just place it.

"They aren't mine," she said to Maginnis. "They belong to Kevin Molton, the man I was with. He brought them from Colombia. I had nothing to do with them."

Maginnis smiled. "I think not, Ms. Odom. Mr. Molton has been working for us on temporary assignment. He undertook this trip with you on our behalf, and he says the cases are yours."

E.B. almost fell off her perch. Kevin Molton? That little twerp? After all she'd done for him. After their more than friendly time together in Colombia. It was unbearable to think about. Of all people, that two-faced loser had ratted her out?

Her face crumpled. She began to cry.

Chapman nudged a box of tissues toward her and waited while she sobbed. Maginnis shifted uneasily from foot to foot.

She dabbed her eyes and turned to Chapman. "May I speak to you in private, please?"

"You'll talk to me," Maginnis said forcefully. "You're in no position to dictate— "

"I can handle this," Chapman said quietly. "It's okay."

"You sure?"

Chapman nodded. "We'll be fine."

"Okay," Maginnis ceded. "But Della stays with you. I'll go check on the others, but I'll be back very shortly, so make it quick." He walked out and closed the door behind him.

E.B.'s eyes welled up. "I suppose you think you and your friends caught me red-handed, as they say. And maybe you have. But you don't understand. I couldn't help myself."

There were more tears. Chapman waited.

"I want you to know that if I did anything wrong, it was because . . . I mean, I'd never have done it on my own. I was forced to, really."

She checked Chapman's expression. His face gave nothing away.

She amped up the tears. "See, after my husband abandoned me, I was helpless and alone. My boss, Mr. Vinson De Theret, it was him. He promised to take care of me if I did everything he wanted. I didn't know what to do. I couldn't help it."

She looked up at Chapman to judge the result of her performance. He had a strange, excited look on his face.

"Interesting story," he said. "Why don't you tell us all about it downtown? We'll take your statement there."

He opened the door and summoned Maginnis.

"Ms. Odom has agreed to tell us all about the De Theret operation," Chapman told him. "I suggest we wrap up here and take this back to the bureau."

Chapman's heart raced as he strode out of the terminal. A tremendous wave of elation poured over him.

He had pursued E.B. Odom as a means to get to Vinson De Theret. If she had taken the fall on her own, his gambit would have been in vain. But his hunch had been correct. She would do anything to save her own skin. De Theret would soon be toast.

Maginnis was waiting for him in the parking area with a puzzled look on his face.

"Something wrong?" Chapman asked.

"Wrong? Uh, no." Maginnis reddened. "I, uh, just wondered how, you know, you did it so fast."

"Got her to confess?"

"Sort of, yeah."

"She seemed to want to. Why?"

"It's just that, when I was in there, she was definitely trying to come on to you. And while I was gone, I looked in on our guy while he was giving his statement." Maginnis looked around and lowered his voice. "You won't believe what Molton is saying about this dame."

"What?"

"Well, he was incredibly relieved that we were here to pick them up. Said he couldn't have survived much more."

Chapman sensed what Maginnis was leading up to, but he played along.

"More what?"

"Molton says she's an incredible turn-on," Maginnis said. "Says she makes you so crazy so fast you can't even think. You just wanna bust your pants with the sexy stuff she throws at you."

Chapman held back a smile. "Really?"

"Yeah," Maginnis said. "But he says the minute you're ready to play, she's at you with those long fingernails. A real screamer, too. Says he's gonna need first aid for the cuts on his back, and maybe a tetanus shot."

"Tetanus?"

"Yeah, and maybe rabies, too." Maginnis's eyes grew round. "You oughta see the place on his shoulder where she bit him."

"You were worried about me?"

Maginnis grinned. "Not worried, exactly. I just didn't want to find you in a compromising position."

Chapman matched his grin. "Guess I'm lucky Della was there to protect me. You should put her in for a commendation, by the way. With all that artillery flying, it was tough duty, for sure."

The agent's face sobered. "Let's get the show on the road before our lady friend changes her mind about cooperating."

Chapman considered the possibility. What if, in the end, E.B. Odom changed her mind and would not testify against De Theret? A hard knot formed in the pit of his stomach. The woman had better come through.

CHAPTER THIRTY-SEVEN

A Guy Named Doyle

The slow stagger of rush hour had Samantha's nerves on fire. Three feet forward. Stop. Two more feet. Stop. The clock on the dashboard of the little red rental car read 5:54. At this rate, even though she could see her destination, she would be late for her six-o'clock rendezvous at Hotel Zaza.

From the hotel's balcony, the view of the verdant, oak-lined boulevards that swirled around and away from the iconic Mecom Fountain below was comparable to some of Europe's finest. But at street level, the heavy traffic that circled the Museum District landmark was a commuter's nightmare.

Three lanes, packed with cars, merged, separated, and merged again as they circled the center knot. From there, vehicles fanned out in all directions—north to Midtown, northwest to The Montrose, south to the Texas Medical Center, southeast to Hermann Park, and east toward the highways that led to the coast.

Samantha maneuvered the rental into a gap between two cars and peeled out of the loop. Around the next corner stood the hotel's entry. She pulled into the valet line behind half a dozen other cars. The place was popular at happy hour.

Two cars back from the door, she stopped the car, dropped her keys into a waiting valet's hand and sped inside.

She wanted to try reaching Carter one last time, but the chic, open lobby offered little privacy. She crossed it quickly and found a quiet space at the far end.

She tried Carter's mobile number. The line went dead before it could connect. She stared at her phone. No signal.

She paced around to find a better spot. Out on the restaurant's terrace, a signal appeared. She tapped Carter's number again. Still no answer. She called the FBI number he'd given her. No luck.

Up until this moment, her idea of posing as a call girl to expose E.B. and Vinson for the scum they were hadn't seemed terribly risky. She had planned every step. After everything was set up, she would alert Carter. He would be angry at first, but he would forgive her, and the FBI would be there to protect her.

At least, that's how it happened in her head. She would wear a wire, and when the crucial moment came, the G-men would bust down the door and save her from a fate worse than death. But she hadn't considered what might happen if she was totally alone and without backup when it came time to spring the trap.

She exhaled deeply and tried to clear her head. *Think.*

If she left now, it would ruin her best chance to help Carter unmask De Theret. If she stayed, maybe she could get through the whole thing unmolested and walk out with enough evidence to hold up in court. These were her choices.

Or, maybe she could get the Doyle guy to cooperate. Maybe he would. She was dressed in a business suit, in case she needed an excuse to fall back on. If things got dicey upstairs, she could claim a scheduling error and say she thought she'd been sent there on real company business.

Maybe Mr. Doyle would be reasonable. Maybe he had a sense of humor and would laugh at the mix-up. No harm done.

She checked her phone. It was past six, and the signal strength that had briefly appeared was gone. Amid the boisterous crowd on the terrace, she found an empty barstool and opened her briefcase. The papers inside would be proof of her intent to talk business.

She located the micro-recorder she sometimes used for business meetings and turned it on, hoping it would pick up incriminating parts of her conversation with Doyle. Before she could change her mind and chicken out, she made her way through the crowd to the elevator.

In the special parking area for law enforcement vehicles at Houston Intercontinental Airport, Carter Chapman slid into the front passenger seat of the black SUV. Della Rhodes took the back seat next to E.B. Odom, who sported government issued bracelets on both wrists.

Mack Maginnis shut the door and started the engine. They drove away from the airport in silence.

Chapman was deep in thought, anticipating on how things would play out once they arrived at the bureau. They were just entering the freeway.

Maginnis slapped his forehead. "I almost forgot, buddy. There's an urgent message for you to call Samantha Newman."

A gasp came from the back seat. Chapman turned his attention momentarily to E.B., who looked as if she had taken ill. "Are you all right?"

"Samantha Newman." Her eyes were slits as they bore into Chapman. "I remember now. You're the guy in the Rolls Royce. I told you I never forget a face."

He returned his attention to Maginnis. "What do you mean, urgent? What did she say?"

Maginnis shrugged. "Just that it was urgent and to call her before six o'clock."

Chapman looked at his watch. It was already after six.

He turned his phone on and checked his messages. One text, a voicemail and more missed calls from Samantha. The tension in her voice worried him. He dialed her number.

No answer. Grasping at straws, he tried the only other number he had.

A young woman answered. "De Theret International."

"Gertrude Gold, please."

"She's probably gone for the day," the receptionist replied. "She usually leaves at five-thirty."

"Could you check, please? This is an emergency."

Chapman was on hold until the phone clicked again.

"Gertrude Gold. May I help you?"

There was no time for pleasantries. "This is Carter Chapman. Do you know where Samantha is?"

"Samantha? No, I don't Mr. Chapman. Isn't she at home?"

"No."

"Is she all right?"

"I don't know. I have an urgent message from her and now I can't find her. I was hoping maybe she called you."

"Sorry. Wish I knew what to tell you."

Chapman wracked his brain for another option. A possibility struck.

"Is Vinson De Theret still in his office?"

"I don't know. Want me to check?"

"Please. Don't connect me. Just tell me if he's there."

Again, he was on hold. Seconds seemed like hours.

"He's gone," Gertie said at last. "But I got his secretary. He has a six o'clock meeting with someone named Doyle at Hotel ZaZa."

He tried to piece the meager information together. "This Doyle guy, do you know him?"

"No," Gertie answered. "Rita says De Theret goes there every week or so to meet him. She's never handled any phone calls or correspondence between them, so she doesn't know what it's about. Only that every so often she'll notice that De Theret has 'Doyle/ZaZa' on his schedule. Do you think Ms. Newman could be there, too?"

"Don't know. But if you hear from her, tell her that's where I'll be."

Chapman asked Maginnis to send an agent to Samantha's house to check things out. Then, with E.B. in tow, they headed for the ZaZa. Even with sirens blaring and lights flashing, at this time of day it could take an hour to get there.

Carter Chapman hoped his concern was unfounded. But the panic he'd heard in Samantha's voice . . .

Was she at the hotel? If so, what for? Was it something to do with her seeing De Theret yesterday?

Damn! He had everything worked out. Why couldn't she just be patient?

CHAPTER THIRTY-EIGHT

Phwock!

The room at Hotel ZaZa, number 432, was miles down the hall. By the time Samantha got close, she was breathless.

The door was ajar. Sounds of Usher crooning to a throbbing electronic beat spilled into the hallway.

She stopped short of the door and tried to reach Chapman one last time. Again, no signal. Maybe a text would get there. With trembling fingers, she managed to type *zaza432* and sent it.

She took a deep breath and knocked on the doorframe.

"Door's open," a voice answered, barely audible over the music.

Her feet were welded to the floor. She called back. "Mr. Doyle?"

"The door's open," came the reply. "Come in!"

Nothing to be done now but forge ahead. She pushed lightly on the door. It swung open to reveal the living room area of an elegant suite, furnished in blacks and golds and expensive-looking furniture. Music filled the space between her and the man at the wet bar across the room. His back was to the door, but she could see that he was working the cork out of a bottle of champagne.

Phwock went the cork. She gasped.

The man turned around. "Didn't scare you, did I?"

Her heart froze in her chest. Before her stood Vinson De Theret.

"You look surprised, Samantha. Come in and shut the door behind you."

There wasn't breath enough to speak, or think. Her legs turned to jelly. She could only wobble forward.

"Let me take your jacket." He crossed the room and slipped it off her shoulders, his eyes playing over the exposed skin of her neck and throat.

Her pulse kicked into overdrive.

He hung her jacket over a chair near the sofa and set her briefcase beside it. She stood in stupefied silence as he returned to the bar, filled two glasses with champagne, and handed one to her.

"Sorry for the little deception. Doyle is an old family name. I use it when it suits me. The people in this hotel know me by it. Cheers!"

He clinked his glass against hers. "Let's have a seat." He took her hand and pulled her down with him to the sofa.

She didn't trust her voice. Maybe by the time she could think of something to say, it would be there.

He placed his pale, freckled hand on her thigh. "I don't always do this. . . audition girls, I mean. Only the ones who interest me. And you interest me, Samantha, more than you know."

His hand felt like a squirming lizard. She jumped up and let it fall to the sofa. An image exploded against her skull. Lista! Had he "auditioned" Lista, too? Is this what happened to her?

She had to get out of there. She stepped away from the sofa, out of arm's reach.

His red-rimmed eyes followed her. "I didn't mean to startle you. I thought you'd be more comfortable getting back in the game with someone familiar. After all, we like each other, don't we? I'm sure you've fantasized about us before. I know I have."

A wave of nausea passed through her. The champagne quivered in her glass, betraying her nerves. She moved farther away toward the window. Below, traffic silently circled the fountain in the thickening dusk.

"Samantha?" He sounded hurt. His eyes began a blinking routine.

Perhaps she wasn't really in danger. She took a deep breath and tried to regain her composure. "It just feels too . . . strange."

"Strange?"

She turned to face him again. "I thought Doyle was just an anonymous person. You're my boss. I . . . I'm more comfortable with strangers. You know, like I told you, no entanglements."

"No entanglements here, Samantha. Just pleasure. I'm a paying customer." He chuckled. "Even if I do get a kickback on the fee."

The fee. She glanced at her briefcase on the chair and wondered if his words were clear enough to register on the recorder inside. She hoped she would get the chance to find out.

She raised her voice as she moved toward the briefcase. "You haven't really explained the fee, Vinson. Aren't I supposed to get the money up front?"

"Normally, yes. New clients pay cash. A regular customer would sign a voucher that you'd turn in for payment. But you haven't got one for me to sign, have you?" He smiled. "We'll take care of it later, when you're officially an Elite Professional employee."

Another shock of recognition: Elite Professionals. Carter was right. No wonder they all dressed like high-priced call girls.

De Theret rose and refilled his glass. "Don't worry, Samantha. You'll be paid for this. The full two grand. It's what our best girls get. I'd never cheat myself out of a commission. Now, let's toast to our new business relationship."

He joined her at the window and clinked his glass against hers. "Drink up, girl! You haven't even taken the first sip. Drink. You'll feel better. You seem a little rusty at this."

She took a sip, unsure if she'd be able to swallow it. But when the slight astringency of the first sip braced her, she gulped down the rest.

"That's better." He took her glass and turned to the bar to refill it.

She used the moment to check the distance between her and her briefcase, and her briefcase and the door. But he was back with the champagne before she could act.

He handed the glass to her. "Now drink this one, too. I want us to have a nice time together. Only thing is, I'm in a bit of a rush. You were late, and E.B.'s plane should be landing about now. She'll be waiting for me to pick her up, and she hates it when I'm late."

Samantha recognized a new escape possibility. "I don't think we should betray E.B. like this, Vinson. It doesn't feel right."

His face turned crimson. "Come on girl, this is business! I shouldn't have to even say that to you. I thought you were a pro. Are you trying to get fired before you start? Or have you been lying to me all along?" He blinked furiously.

"Lying?" She tried to sound indignant. "I'm not lying. Didn't you talk to Angelo Infante about me? I didn't ask for this job. You insisted, remember?"

That's it, she thought. If I argue with him and make this a huge fight, I can storm out with my briefcase. I'll be safe. And I'll have the whole thing recorded. Real evidence for the FBI, and for Carter.

She amped up the anger until she was practically yelling. "How could you accuse me of lying to you, after all these years, Vinson? You know I'm a professional! I don't have to take your insults."

She made a move to grab her case.

De Theret caught her by the arm. "You're not leaving until we work this out."

She tried to pull away.

His grip tightened. "Do not walk out on me."

He was stronger than she realized. There had to be a better way to end this. She stopped struggling.

He let her go. "Let's sit down for a minute and enjoy the time we have."

Her head screamed. *Run!* But she couldn't leave without the proof in the briefcase. He was too close to it now for her to grab it.

His voice turned silky and intimate. "I understand. You're a little uncomfortable. I wasn't entirely up front with you, and I apologize for that. And I'm sorry I accused you of lying. Let's forget it and move forward." He returned to the sofa and patted the cushion beside him. "Come sit."

She remained at the window, calculating her next move.

"All right, stay there, if you like. I have something in the other room for you." He stood and disappeared into the bedroom.

Now. Grab the briefcase *now*.

She made a move toward the table, but he was back before she could reach the case. She dropped to the sofa and tried to look calm, hoping he hadn't seen the mad dash.

He sat beside her and laid a silky red bag on her lap. "I want you to put this on."

She stared at the bag, not moving.

He opened the bag himself and withdrew a miniscule silk thong trimmed in fur. His fingers played over it, gently stroking the fur. "I'm told it's very stimulating."

Her pulse banged against her skull as she gaped at the disgusting pelt.

"I bought this today, Samantha, especially for you. It's soft and lush, like you are. Of course, I care for E.B., but you will please me in a different way, I'm sure. Take off your clothes, and I'll help you put it on."

She wouldn't be able to think if she panicked now. She willed herself to breathe.

An idea formed. She jumped up again. "I'll put it on myself, Vinson. It will just be a minute." Before he could protest, she grabbed the fur piece and went for her briefcase.

De Theret stood up and blocked her path. "Where are you going?"

"To the bathroom. I have things I need in my case."

"You don't need anything more than what I gave you." He grabbed the briefcase from her and flung it away. "And I told you, I want to put it on you. I like to see everything I'm getting. Participation is a must."

She was out of options. And paralyzed with fear.

"I've waited years for you, Samantha. I've been a complete gentleman, haven't I?" He stroked her shoulders and ran his hands down her arms. "You always seemed so special, so . . . virginal. And that's how I'll treat you, gently, like the little girl you'll always be to me. I like the way you've hesitated to come to me. It makes me want you even more."

He pulled her to him. His damp breath tickled her neck.

"No!" She pushed him away with all her strength. He stumbled backward over the marble table and fell to the floor, dazed.

Panic rose in her like a volcano. She raked her eyes over the room in search of her briefcase. It was not in sight.

De Theret was struggling to right himself. Before he recovered, she needed something to defend herself with. Her eyes locked onto the champagne bottle.

He had seen it, too. Faster than she imagined, he jumped up and grabbed her arm just as her fingers closed around the bottle's neck. He wrestled it away and shoved her against the wall. Enraged, he swung the bottle at her.

She ducked and drove her head into his stomach and pounded both fists into his crotch as hard as she could. He roared and doubled over, then fell backward over the table again. The bottle cracked open against the marble. Champagne spewed everywhere.

Frantic, she scoured the room for her briefcase, but before she could locate it, he was staggering toward her, wielding the broken bottle.

"No!!!" Her scream reverberated against the walls. *Bang!*

Something across the room exploded. Then suddenly, everything was terrifyingly still. Not a sound, except the thumping beat of the music.

De Theret's eyes were transfixed like a hare caught in the headlights of an oncoming truck. He was staring past her, toward the door to the hallway.

She followed his gaze. Her heart was pumping so fast, her brain was slow to register what had happened.

The door seemed to be off its hinges. In the open doorframe stood a man pointing a gun. Behind him in the hallway were other people with guns drawn.

The man in the doorway stepped into the room. "Get away from him, Samantha. Walk away."

The sound of his voice snapped everything into focus, but she was trembling too violently to move. "Carter? Carter, I—"

Two other men rushed inside. One of them grabbed De Theret.

Carter Chapman took her in his arms and pulled her tight against him.

She couldn't stop shivering, even with his warmth surrounding her.

"It's all right now. It's over," he whispered. "You're safe."

His embrace eased her panic. She had come through. She had won. So had Lista, and Derek. And Carter, too.

Relief poured through her like warm brandy, and when it reached her heart, she sobbed.

CHAPTER THIRTY-NINE

Mystery Guest

A late spring breeze warmed the Central Texas countryside. Rich, deep hues of bluebonnets and Indian paintbrush that had thrilled Samantha on her last visit were giving way to swaths of buttery yellow coreopsis.

She joined the group gathered on the broad veranda at Carter Chapman's ranch as they raised their glasses in a toast.

"To Serenity!"

Gertie took a sip of bubbly. "If I had a place like this, I'd never leave."

Maginnis swigged the last of the beer from his bottle. "Me either. Wish my FBI pension came with digs like this. Chapman, you're a lucky sumbitch."

"I don't know," Kevin Molton commented from his chair next to Gertie. "I mean, it's nice and all, but there isn't much action around here, y'know?"

Gertie gave him an exasperated look. "My dear nephew, haven't you had enough action lately?"

Molton blushed.

Maginnis exchanged a glance with Carter and grinned. "Hey, Chapman, I'm told you keep horses around here."

Carter refilled Gertie's wine glass and sat beside Samantha. "We could go for a trail ride after lunch, if you're up to it."

Maginnis stood. "Well, I think I'll just take a quick mosey down to the stable right now and select my steed before you other guys get your dibs. C'mon, Molton, let's take a walk."

Happy to escape, Molton rose and followed Maginnis toward the horse barn.

Samantha smiled at Gertie. "You were kind of rough on Kevin just now."

"Rough?" Gertie shook her head. "That young man never had it rough. My sister has spoiled him from Day One. I love him to pieces, but you know what a pain in the neck he can be."

"I think he'll be fine," Carter commented.

"Hmmph," Gertie sniffed. You don't know the amount of convincing it took. At first, he wouldn't believe what I was telling him about the drugs and everything else. He didn't want to ruin his big chance for advancement. I had to practically hit him over the head with a two-by-four to explain that he wasn't going to have a company to advance in for very long, and that if he didn't work with you, he'd probably wind up in prison out of sheer stupidity."

"He just needs a little maturing," Carter countered. "He's bright enough, and with a little guidance, he could be a valuable company man."

"You have a company in mind?" Gertie asked. "Maybe they have a job for me, too."

"I think Mack plans to talk to him about the training program at the Bureau. After all, he came through pretty well on his first assignment. But now that you mention it, Mrs. Gold, I've been thinking about hiring someone myself. Why don't you come work for me?"

"What would I be doing?" Gertie leaned forward, her eyes wide. "Any undercover business?"

He laughed. "Well, I already know you can keep a secret. But I was thinking more along the lines of what you did for Samantha. You know, organizing my appointment schedule, working with a couple of charities I'm involved with, keeping track of my consulting contracts. Although you will need security clearance for some of those." No skeletons in your closet, I hope."

Gertie blushed. "Would you need me to relocate? I mean, it's pretty here, but—"

The honk of a car's horn cut through the air. The three on the veranda turned to see a white SUV billowing dust behind it as it negotiated the drive up to the house.

Samantha turned to Carter. "Expecting someone else?"

"A last-minute guest."

"Who?"

"As it turns out, he's a little surprise for you, Samantha."

Puzzled, she squinted at the car. It came to a stop in front of the house. The driver's door opened, and out stepped a man of medium height, athletic build, and thinning sandy brown hair.

She studied him as he strode toward the house. He wore a tan safari shirt and jeans and carried a canvas backpack over one shoulder. He did not look familiar.

Carter waved at the visitor. "Over here! Turn left at the top of the steps."

The man returned the wave.

Samantha was baffled. "Am I supposed to know him?"

Carter chuckled. "Yes, and no."

She turned to Gertie. "Do you know who he is?"

"Haven't the foggiest."

When the visitor neared their table, Carter rose to greet him. The two men embraced warmly, slapping each other on the back.

"Samantha, Gertie, I'd like you to meet my old college roommate, Roland Dabney, a most excellent producer for the ever-popular television show, News Journal Reports. Rollo, this is Gertie and Sam."

Gertie shook his hand. "I think we've spoken on the phone before."

"We certainly have." Dabney spoke with a distinct Nu Yawk accent. "Pleasure to meet you."

"You're the real Roland Dabney?" Samantha studied his face. "I believe you once stood me up, sir."

Dabney laughed. "But I sent my proxy. Although, had I known what I was missing, I would've shown up myself."

Carter jumped in. "Oh, no you don't! You're a married man. No flirting allowed."

Dabney looked around, taking in the view. "Nice place you have here, old pal. Not bad, for Texas."

"We do our best," Carter replied. "Have a seat and partake."

"Actually, I have something to discuss with you," Dabney said. "Ladies, would you excuse us for a few minutes."

Carter frowned. "I thought this was only a social visit."

Dabney looked intently at Carter. "The news never stops."

Dottie appeared from the kitchen. "Lunch is ready, if you are."

Carter stood. "We have a couple of strays out at the stables, and Mr. Dabney and I will be upstairs for a short while. Let's wait a few minutes before we call everyone to table."

Dottie nodded and huffed back to the kitchen. Carter and Dabney also disappeared inside.

Gertie stood and poured herself another glass of champagne. "What is that about, I wonder?"

Samantha's mind traveled to Carter's locked room on the third floor. He and Dabney were likely meeting up there now.

She recognized Dabney's voice as the caller from News Journal Reports who'd set up her first meeting with Carter. It seemed like eons ago.

Now, here was Dabney in the flesh. It was obvious the men were more than just old college roommates. They were colleagues of some sort.

It occurred to her that she didn't really know what Carter's life was like, or what it would be, now that De Theret was dealt with. Or even what her life would become, for that matter.

Gertie's voice snapped her back to the veranda.

"Do you think Mr. Chapman was serious about offering me a job? I wonder what it would be like, working for him. I bet he's into more than just software consulting, if you know what I mean."

Samantha took a sip of champagne. "Everybody has secrets. If you go to work for him, you'll know all of his. Then you can tell me."

"Well, I suppose it could be interesting, working for a man like that. If it's not too dangerous."

"Believe me, he won't put anyone he likes in danger. I speak from experience."

"But you were in danger, Samantha. You were almost killed!"

"That was my fault, not his. I was stupid to try something like that alone. Won't happen again."

"Again? I should hope not!"

Samantha smiled. She would miss Gertie's daily presence in her life. If Carter hired her, and if their feelings for one another deepened, maybe she wouldn't have to.

Her cell phone buzzed. She checked the caller ID and answered. "Hello, Angel!"

She excused herself and moved toward a corner of the veranda to continue the conversation. As usual with the Angel, it was brief. She returned to the table to see a question forming on Gertie's face.

"Was that a friend calling?"

Samantha nodded.

"Do I know her?"

"Him."

"I heard you call him Angel. Do you have another boyfriend I didn't know about?"

"Oh no, just a good friend. A guardian angel, you could say. He was checking to make sure I was okay."

"Speaking of secrets." Gertie shook her head. "I've worked for you a long time, Samantha, but after all that's happened, I'm not sure I know all of your secrets, either." She was about to ask another question, but Samantha stopped her.

"Aren't you taking this sleuthing business a little too seriously, Miss Nosey-Pants?"

Gertie blushed. "If I'm going to work for Mr. Chapman, I need to practice!"

Dottie appeared again, carrying an old iron triangle and beater. She stopped at the top of the porch steps and struck the triangle, calling everyone to the table.

A minute later, Maginnis and Molton reappeared on the path from the stables and slowly made their way up to the house. By the time they rejoined the two women on the veranda, there was still no sign of Carter and Dabney.

"I've been smelling whatever's in that smoker since I got here," Maginnis said. He and Molton sat down. "And I'm prepared to make a pig of myself."

Dottie reappeared with a heavy tray of food. She set it on the table, filled the glasses with iced tea and returned to the kitchen for a fresh beer for Maginnis, just as Carter and Dabney emerged from the house.

"Pull up a chair, Rollo," Carter said as they approached the table. "You're about to meet some real Texas barbeque. Probably better than you deserve."

Amid platefuls of barbequed ribs and brisket, fresh corn-on-the-cob, cole slaw and black-eyed peas, the company sat in the shade of the big house, talking about show biz gossip, politics, and the economy. But the friendly chitchat did not take Samantha's mind off Carter's impromptu meeting with Dabney.

Though their faces held no hint of the nature of their conversation, Samantha sensed a fresh strain in Carter's outwardly cheerful demeanor. What the source of it was, she hadn't a clue.

CHAPTER FORTY

Disappeared

Dottie emerged from the house to clear the table.
"Hope you folks saved room for dessert," Carter said, "because we're in for a treat. Right Dottie?"

"Don't go buildin' it up," she replied. "Let them be the judge." She disappeared inside with a tray full of empty plates.

Molton turned to Maginnis. "What will happen to Vinson and E.B. now?"

"Who cares?" Gertie blurted. "Good riddance to bad rubbish." She drank down the rest of her champagne.

Dabney's cell phone buzzed. He pulled it from his pocket and excused himself from the table.

Maginnis leaned forward to answer Molton's question. "We've got E.B. Odom dead to rights on drug trafficking, thanks to you. And we picked up her husband yesterday."

Samantha sat up. "Trey Odom? He's alive?"

"Not Odom," Maginnis said. "He died last year in a plane crash near Bogotá. Probably not an accident, by the way. The guy we collared yesterday likely had something to do with that, and the blast that killed Derek Grey."

"But Trey Odom was E.B.'s husband," Gertie said. "Wasn't he?"

"Poor guy probably thought so," Maginnis said. "But she never divorced the first one."

Dabney's call ended. He returned to the table and whispered something to Carter, then spoke to the group.

"Excuse me, folks, duty calls." He disappeared into the house.

Carter turned to Samantha. "Wait ten minutes, then meet me in the library."

Alone together in the library, Samantha searched Carter's face for a clue to what was happening.

His eyes held the familiar sadness. "I have to go away for a few days. I wish I could explain, but I can't, except to say that I'm sorry to run out on you like this. I was going to tell you after everyone left, but I have to leave sooner than I thought."

"But . . . where . . . how—?"

Dabney poked his head in. "Sorry to rush you, but we've got a plane to catch."

Carter took Samantha's hands in his. "With any luck, I'll be back in a few days."

"I don't understand."

"Dottie and Ralph and the kids are here. Stick around, get to know the place better while I'm gone."

She pulled away. "Get to know the place? I've just discovered that I don't know you like I thought I did. What am I supposed to—?"

Dabney opened the door again. "We have to go, man. Now."

Carter pressed a folded-up piece of notepaper into her palm. "I thought I'd have more time for this, but it's as far as I got. You can read it later. There's something else for you upstairs. Maybe it'll occupy you for a while."

He kissed her on the forehead and touched her cheek softly. "I'll make it up to you, I promise."

She closed her eyes, savoring his touch. When she opened them, he was gone.

She heard him talking to the group outside. Before long, Dabney's car rattled to life. Soon, the engine's rumble faded.

Samantha lingered in the library, a million questions flooding her thoughts. She stared at the note in her hand. Carter had said to read it later, but she couldn't wait.

Unfolded, the note revealed a short, hand-written message. *Here's another corny joke for you,* it read.

What do you call a camel at the North Pole?

Just what she needed. One more riddle from the man who had just abandoned her. Hoping for more, she turned the note over.

One word completed the riddle.

Lost.

Underneath was a postscript:

And that's how I feel without you.

Tears sprang in her eyes. She blotted them with the back of her hand and dropped the note into her pocket.

She had no idea how long she'd been standing there when she heard someone calling her name from the veranda.

"Dessert's on the table," Dottie announced as she passed by the library door. "They're asking for you."

Whatever excuse Carter had used for his sudden departure seemed to have left his guests unworried. Over wedges of chocolate coconut pie, the animated conversation about the abrupt demise of De Theret International continued.

"Samantha!" Gertie was flush with excitement. "Wait 'til you hear about E.B. Odom's first husband!"

Maginnis picked up the story. "The guy was some punk she'd run off with when she was a girl. He did time in prison for a while, long enough for her to find hubby number two. When number one found out, he demanded money to keep quiet. Once he got paroled, she hired him every so often to do her dirty work. Turns out, he was the car mechanic that set the bomb in Ms. Newman's car."

Samantha was stunned. *Derek's killer!*

Gertie reached for her hand. "They got him, dear. They got them all."

The table went quiet until Samantha found her voice. "All but one. The one who murdered Lista."

"We're close," Maginnis said. "They're testing DNA as we speak. Won't be long 'til we nab him."

There would be no rest for Samantha until Lista's murderer faced justice. At least E.B. Odom was out of her life for good. She'd be happy to never hear the woman's name again. Or any mention of Vinson De Theret and his corrupt De Theret International.

As the conversation buzzed around her, Samantha's attention returned to Carter's note. She wondered if she'd missed something in it. She pulled it out of her pocket and reread it.

She had. In one corner a short series of numbers had been scribbled: 81625.

At first glance, they seemed meaningless. Her brain started working, trying to arrange the digits into something that made sense. Too short for a phone number. A birthday? August 16, 1925. Nothing clicked. Lotto numbers, maybe? But why would he be giving her lotto numbers?

She couldn't remember anything he'd said or done that would have prepared her for his sudden departure. Now she had only questions without answers.

81625, 81625. . .

She itched to dash upstairs to find whatever else Carter had left for her there. It could be a clue to the numbers on his note.

She forced her attention back to the people at the table.

Kevin Molton was speaking. "Roland Dabney's kind of interesting. I never met a television producer before. Must be an exciting job, not knowing where a story will take you. Wish I could've gone with them."

"Be careful what you wish for," Maginnis commented. "No telling what those two might be up to."

The conversation circled around the table, but Samantha's mind had moved elsewhere. She pulled her phone from her pocket and typed the numbers from the note into the browser.

81625. Zip code for Craig, Colorado?

She clicked the map in the listing. Craig, Colorado seemed to be in the middle of nowhere, closer to Wyoming than it was to Denver. Elk hunting was big there, apparently. Is that where Carter was headed?

Dottie appeared with a tray of fresh glasses and a bottle of dark wine.

"Mr. Chapman wanted y'all to try this. She set the tray down in front of Samantha. "It's a local number, port wine from Messina Hof, just up the road from here."

Dottie's words sparked something in Samantha's brain. Local number. . . up the. . .

As her mind traveled up to the third floor, she had an idea.

Maginnis stood and poured the wine for everyone. He gulped his down and set the empty glass on the table with a thud. "Guess that means lunch is over. Time to go riding."

Gertie drained her glass. "Off into the shunshet!" She hiccupped. "Oopsh, between the two glashes of champagne and thish one, I think I'm a little tipshy!"

Molton put his arm around her shoulder. "Sure you're okay to ride, Aunt Gertie?"

She huffed. "'Coursh I am. Wouldn't have the nerve to get on a horsh if I weren't shmashed!"

She tried to stand but failed and plopped into her chair. Molton helped her up again.

She took a wobbly step forward. "Oopsh. Shamantha! I forgot to tell you. That Dabney guy wansh to interview us about the whole De Theret thing for his TV show when he getsh back."

"Did he say when that would be?"

Gertie was too focused on negotiating the porch steps to answer. Molton held on to her as she wobbled onto solid ground. "Aren't you coming, Shamantha?"

"You guys go ahead. I have to run upstairs."

As soon as the trio found the path to the horse stable, Samantha made a mad dash inside and fairly flew up the staircase to the third floor.

The door to Carter's inner sanctum was locked, as Samantha expected. Her hand shook as she entered the digits into the keypad. 81625. Nothing. Perhaps she had entered it wrong. She tried again, forward and backward. Still nothing.

The numbers obviously weren't the security code.

Perhaps Carter hadn't meant for her to climb all the way up when he said 'upstairs.' Whatever he left for her could be on the second floor, in his bedroom. She turned to go there.

As she started down the staircase, she heard a noise behind her.

"Ms. Newman?"

Ralph Velasco, Carter's go-to guy at Serenity, stood in the open doorway. He must have seen her through the surveillance cameras. Or heard her clumsy attempt to get through the door.

Her face heated. "I wasn't trying to break in or anything. I know this place is off limits. It's just that Carter said he left something for me upstairs and I thought he meant—"

"He left it with me. Wait here." He backed inside the room and shut the door.

Her heart raced in anticipation.

In less than ten seconds, the door was open again. Ralph handed her an envelope. In it was a single sheet of paper.

It was a type-written list of things to do around Serenity Ranch, complete with directions, and the mobile phone numbers for Ralph and Dottie if she needed them.

Carter had scrawled *Please stay* at the bottom.

Nice, though she couldn't help feeling let down.

Questions swirled in her head. Maybe Ralph would answer a few.

"Do you know where Carter went?"

Ralph shrugged.

She tried again. "How long will he be gone?"

"Sorry, but even if I knew, I couldn't say.

With no other recourse, Samantha thanked him for the note and turned to leave.

"Ms. Newman?"

She turned to face him again. "Yes?"

"Mr. Chapman did say that you'd probably be curious about this room. Said I could let you in, if you wanted. Only for a minute, though."

A peek into Serenity's inner sanctum was too tempting to refuse. At least it might put her a step closer to solving the mystery of Carter Chapman.

She nodded.

"Here you go, then." Ralph opened the door, and Samantha stepped inside.

THE END

ABOUT THE AUTHOR

Gay Yellen has been sneezed on by an elephant, held at gunpoint, and survived a killer California earthquake, which may explain her penchant for writing cliffhangers.

She began her working life as an actress, then moved behind the camera at The American Film Institute (AFI) as Assistant to the Director of Production.

A former magazine editor and national journalism award winner, she was the contributing book editor for *Five Minutes to Midnight* (Delacorte), an international thriller.

Gay lives in Texas. She loves connecting with readers, book clubs and other groups in person and online. You can reach her through her website, GayYellen.com.

Acknowledgments

My mother transcribed a poem into my baby book which she claimed I composed around the age of three. Prose came later. I'm forever grateful to my parents for filling our home with love and literature.

The spirit of Shirley Wiley, my high school English teacher, still informs my writing. As I work, I imagine her spot-on comments at the margins of my pages, encouraging me to always look for the truest word.

I'm grateful to Roger Paulding for his enthusiasm for the first draft of *The Body Business*, and to the members of his Houston Writers Guild critique group who embraced the manuscript and helped me work out the kinks.

Thanks to Heidi Wolens Hancock for her intelligence and candor, and for allowing me to experience this first solo novel coming to life in a reader's imagination. And to Jackie Mazow, for her support in everything I do.

Many thanks to Pamela Fagan Hutchins and SkipJack Publishing for embracing this new edition of Book 1 of The Samantha Newman Mystery Series.

Deep gratitude to my remarkable husband, Donald Reiser, for sharing his love of the history of Central Texas with me. His appreciation for the beauty of the region inspired me to imagine Serenity Ranch.

And thanks to my readers, who said they wanted more.

The Samantha Newman Mysteries
by Gay Yellen

The Body Business
The Body Next Door
The News Body (Winter 2020-2021)

Other books from SkipJack Publishing
Murder, They Wrote: Four SkipJack Mysteries,
by Pamela Fagan Hutchins,
Ken Oder, R.L. Nolen, and Marcy Mason
The Closing, by Ken Oder
Old Wounds to the Heart, by Ken Oder
The Judas Murders, by Ken Oder
The Princess of Sugar Valley, by Ken Oder
Pennies from Burger Heaven, by Marcy McKay
Stars Among the Dead, by Marcy McKay
The Moon Rises at Dawn, by Marcy McKay
Bones and Lies Between Us, by Marcy McKay
Deadly Thyme, by R. L. Nolen
The Dry, by Rebecca Nolen
Tides of Possibility, edited by K.J. Russell
Tides of Impossibility, edited by K.J. Russell and C.
Stuart Hardwick
*My Dream of Freedom: From Holocaust to My Beloved
America,* by Helen Colin

Now that you've finished The Body Business
Please consider taking a moment to leave a brief
review on the book's Amazon , BookBub or
Goodreads page. It's a great way to help other readers
know if they might enjoy the book, too. Thank you!

Want to know more about Gay Yellen?

Follow Gay on
Amazon
BookBub
Facebook
Twitter
Instagram

For inside info and news about Gay's books, sign up at
GayYellen.com.

Made in the USA
Columbia, SC
22 July 2022